Hercules X-Posed

TED EDWARDS

Hercules X-Posed

The Unauthorized Biography of Kevin Sorbo and His On-Screen Character

PRIMA PUBLISHING

Library of Congress Cataloging-in-Publication Data

Edwards, Ted.
Hercules x-posed : the unauthorized biography of Kevin Sorbo and his on-screen character / by Ted Edwards.
p. cm.
Includes index.
ISBN 0-7615-1366-3
1. Kevin Sorbo 2. Hercules, the legendary journeys (Television Program) I. Title.
PN1992.77.H44E38 1998 97-52952
791.45'72—dc21 CIP

98 99 00 01 02 DD 10 9 8 7 6 5 4 3 2 1
Printed in the United States of America

To Barbara Post

We Miss You

Contents

CONTENTS

CONTENTS

INTRODUCTION

BEING A LONGTIME FAN OF *STAR TREK*, IT WAS WITH SOME DISMAY that I noticed the rising ratings of the syndicated series *Hercules: The Legendary Journeys.* That dismay turned to slack jawed shock when the series actually passed *Deep Space Nine* in the Nielsens.

I had caught a moment of *Hercules* here or there, and, to be perfectly honest, I wasn't all that impressed.

Still, I reasoned, there had to be *something* there that I was missing. It's a situation I'd been in before, particularly with a show called *Wiseguy,* which I had refused to watch during its debut season and only caught on summer reruns after being hounded by a couple of friends to do so. The result? I became absolutely hooked on the show.

With *Wiseguy* in mind, I decided to give *Hercules* a fair shake. Sitting down for a couple of episodes, I began to understand what it was about the show that was so appealing to people. On the surface, it's a fairly goofy exercise, but what I discovered is that if you allow yourself to relax and step down from your high-and-mighty platform for a while, you'll be swept up in a wave of magic. Suddenly, I was ten years old again, staying up on Saturday nights to watch *Creature Feature* on WNEW Channel 5 in New York and thrilling to not only the classic Universal horror films but also the efforts of special effects maestro Ray Harryhausen. I was mentally revisiting *Jason and the Argonauts, The Seven Voyages of Sinbad, The Valley of Gwangi, The Beast from 20,000 Fathoms,* and so many more.

In many ways, *Hercules: The Legendary Journeys* was like going home again—warm and nostalgic, without anyone taking anything too seriously. The bottom line is that the show is designed to be fun, and if those are its only ambitions, then it achieves them wonderfully.

Like any successful television series, Herc has inspired a variety of imitators, such as *The Adventures of Sinbad, Conan: The Adventurer,* and even TNT's *Robin Hood* (in which, for the first time, the dude with the arrows is going up against all kinds of bizarre creatures). The truth is that although many of them have attempted to recapture the glossier aspects of *Hercules,* not one has been able to generate its magic or appeal to the audience in the same way.

No surprise there.

The book you're reading is designed to serve as an introduction to the legendary televised journeys of Hercules. As such, it brings you up close and personal with series star, Kevin Sorbo, and offers a behind-the-scenes episode guide to the show's first three seasons.

For making this book a reality, I'd like to thank two people in particular, without whom it most definitely would *not* have been possible: John Schulian, a friend since his days on *Wiseguy,* spent many more hours than he expected to discussing the first forty-eight episodes of *Hercules* (and I still think that, in the end, he got a raw deal from the show), and Bob Bielak, who also spent a tremendous amount of time talking Greek with me. If you enjoy the series, these two gentlemen are undoubtedly a large part of the reason why.

I'd also like to thank my editor at Prima Publishing, Paula Lee, who assigned me this project and then resigned from the company (hopefully there wasn't a connection); Allen Lane for busting his behind and getting me tapes of the various episodes; and my wife, Eileen, for taking our three sons away for a weekend so that I could have a final editorial "push."

So slip on your sandals, pick up your sword, and let's get moving. We're going to the ultimate toga party.

SYGMA/F. TRAPPER

Hercules *star Kevin Sorbo pauses for a photo at the premier of* Kull: The Conqueror.

AP/WIDE WORLD PHOTOS

Minnesota native and Hercules *star, Kevin Sorbo, donated his 1977 high school yearbook as well as items from his film,* Kull: The Conqueror, *to Planet Hollywood Mall of America on Thursday, August 21, 1997.*

SYGMA

Kevin Sorbo takes a moment between the scenes of his hit show, Hercules: The Legendary Journeys, *to chat with one of his fellow actors.*

SYGMA/Gregory Pace

Owing to the widespread success of his hit television show, Kevin Sorbo was a featured guest at the 1997 NATPE convention in New Orleans.

SYGMA/F. Trapper

Kevin Sorbo rides among adoring fans at the 1997 premier of his first full-length motion picture, Kull: The Conqueror.

AP/Wide World Photos

With help from a couple of young ladies, Kevin Sorbo adds his hand prints to the Planet Hollywood Wall of Fame on Thursday, January 8, 1997.

Hercules X-Posed

THE MAN WHO WOULD BE HERC

A Profile of Kevin Sorbo

TELEVISION IS A STRANGE ANIMAL, AND THOSE WHO PLAY IN ITS electronic sandbox have a chance for superstardom or, more likely, obscurity, moving from one show to another and desperately praying that lightning will strike some day.

For the select few, however, the experience is life altering. Through circumstances beyond anyone's imagination, the right actor in the right show strikes a chord with the television audience, and in the synergy that represents so much of the medium, the audience, in turn, elevates the performer to something larger than life. The result is that the performer and the character that he or she portrays becomes nothing short of a phenomenon.

This is especially true in the science fiction and fantasy genres, where a character can *really* hook into an audience and trigger a fervor that is both unmatched and, usually, shorter lived than mainstream television. Among those who have fallen into this category are George Reeves as Superman, Adam West as Batman, Jonathan Frid as vampire Barnabas Collins in the daytime soap *Dark Shadows,* the entire cast of the original *Star Trek,* and, more recently, Ron Perlman as Vincent, the lion-man from *Beauty and the Beast.* Others are Adrian Paul as immortal warrior Duncan MacLeod in *Highlander;* David Duchovny and Gillian Anderson as, respectively, FBI agents Mulder and Scully in *The X-Files;* Lucy Lawless as Xena, Warrior Princess; and, of course, Kevin Sorbo as the demigod Hercules in *The Legendary Journeys.*

The challenge for the actor, naturally, is to take a small-screen phenomenon and translate that success to the big screen, trading Nielsens for the box office. It is *not* an easy thing to do. Just ask Shelly Long, David Caruso, George Clooney, or the cast of *Friends.* Often it's because the audience doesn't want to see actors and actresses stray from their most well-known characterizations, or the performers have gone so far in the opposite direction of their TV roles that they've lost their audiences completely.

In Kevin Sorbo's case, when he had the opportunity to make the leap to feature films, he attempted to find a balance that would bridge the gap between the screens. In fact, when Sorbo returned to the New Zealand set of *Hercules: The Legendary Journeys* to commence production on the fourth season of the hit syndicated series, he was feeling confident in his choice of a feature film debut, *Kull: The Conqueror,* based on the Robert E. Howard character.

Although the original screenplay for the film written by Charles Edward Pogue was a dark and extremely bloody exercise that would have guaranteed an R or NC-17 rating, once the actor was cast, producer Rafaella De Laurentiis decided to lighten things up considerably, shifting the character closer in tone to television's Hercules than the original conception of Conan's father, Kull.

"Why pick *Kull* as your first feature?" Sorbo mused accurately, unable to deny the logic of the question, given the fact that he had wrapped up the third season of *Hercules,* starred in the sword-and-fantasy feature, and segued *back* into Herc's leather pants without a break. "I've probably reached the insane point," he laughed. "I'm ready to chop off this hair and play a Marine Sergeant. I'm *ready* for something different, but the truth is that I still enjoy doing *Hercules.* I'm having a ball with it, though I understand the question."

According to the thirty-eight-year-old actor, he was offered three scripts during hiatus, and the only one that appealed to him was *Kull,* helped in no small way by the fact that the film was a Universal production, the studio that happened to own the series as well. As such, it would make the shuffling of schedules considerably easier than it might have been. Indeed, the film overlapped by three weeks the show's commencement of production, and Sorbo didn't sweat the situation at all.

"What it really came down to," he explained, "is that I said, 'Look, for the first film maybe I should do something that's somewhat similar to *Hercules.*' They're actually quite different, but I can understand why people are going to make comparisons. It just made sense to do something that would, hopefully, bring the *Hercules* audience to the movies. The characters are actually quite different. Kull is a much darker guy, although I can say fans of the character—and I'll go on the record with this—are going to be disappointed. We purposely geared the film so that kids could still go. We got a PG-13 rating, whereas the original script was a definite R if not an X because of the violence. There was just graphic violence, which is what Kull is and what he was, and the film is probably going to alienate the really hardcore fans. For that I apologize."

Kull originally began as *Conan III,* but when Arnold Schwarzenegger—after a year of debate—passed on the project, it shifted to Howard's other most famous creation, who also happens to be Conan's father. In the film, Kull attempts to reclaim his throne from the recently arisen goddess Akivasha, who uses black magic and manipulated mortals to combat him.

Screenwriter Pogue is well-known for his darker, more psychological scripts (the remake of *The Fly, D.O.A.,* and *Psycho III,* among others) as well as his ongoing battle to preserve the writer's efforts when a script is brought to the screen. Unfortunately, it's a battle he has often lost, helplessly watching while multitiered stories and intricate characterizations are whittled down to the lowest common denominator. It happened most recently with *Dragonheart* and, in his opinion, again in the Dan Mancini rewrite of *Kull.* Sorbo admitted that although he was aware of the situation, he couldn't apologize for it.

"I'm sure he's not going to like the film," said Sorbo of Pogue matter-offactly. "I understand writers. They want to see what they wrote brought to the screen, but for as long as movies have been made, there are very few writers who have been happy with the final results. That's just part of the business. There are too many cooks in the kitchen, so to speak. But I think it's a fun film. We lightened up some areas and let the adlibbing thing sort of happen, which I love doing. Kull is a darker hero, and this film has a different look than a lot of others. Just to shoot in Croatia and Slovakia and being in these old countries and shooting in structures that are thousands of years old was incredible. You know, if this film is another obstacle I've got to overcome in terms of people saying, 'Oh look, that's all he can do,' so be it.

"Hollywood is an interesting business," he understated. "There's a billion people who want to be actors and only a few who are able to get a break and make it. It's easier to tell somebody they're never going to make it. I've lived it all my life. I spent fifteen years of my life with people saying I should fall back on my marketing and advertising degrees and get a 'real' job. Well, that just fueled the fire for me. I said, 'Screw that. This is what I want, and I'm going to make it.' I don't want this to sound egotistical, but the truth is I always believed I would work in this business. There was nothing else I wanted to do. I honestly believe that when I tell people to follow their dreams, that when you do follow them, they will come true. It is a matter of how persistent you are. My family has always been supportive. I spent a lot of time doing what most actors have to do—going through the rejection process and the frustration and wondering why you are even attempting to go after this career. But they were always behind me, and I think they are quite proud. I really believe that it comes down to believing in yourself because who else is going to believe in me? If people want to pigeonhole me, that's just one more thing you've got to prove to people. I believe in my abilities. I believe I can play a black pregnant woman, so leave me alone."

The actor was born Kevin David Sorbo on September 24, 1958, in Mound, Minnesota (a suburb of Minneapolis), to Lynn and Ardis Sorbo, a

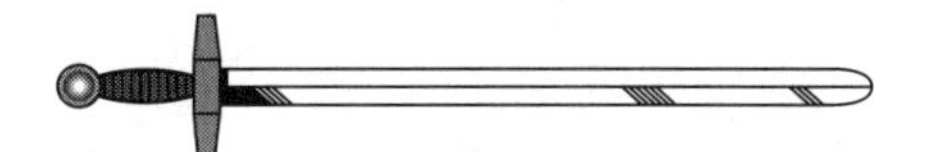

"I've probably reached the insane point. I'm ready to chop off this hair and play a Marine Sergeant."

—Kevin Sorbo

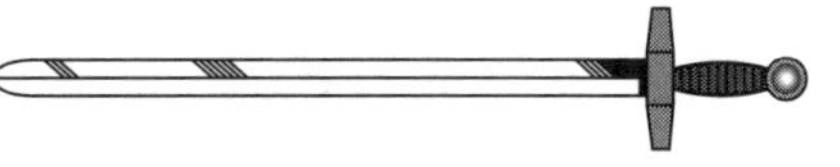

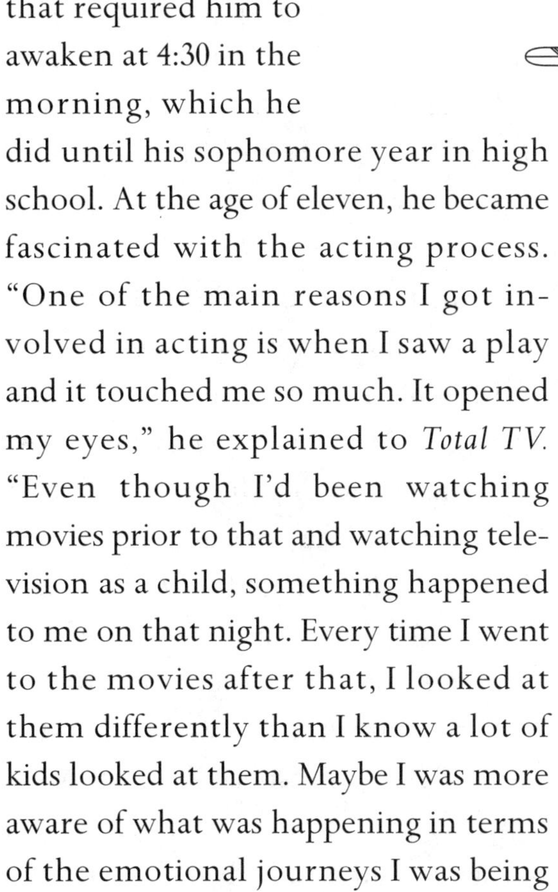

junior high school teacher and a nurse, respectively. The fourth of five children (three brothers and one sister), he attended Shirley Hills grade school. He acquired a paper route that required him to awaken at 4:30 in the morning, which he did until his sophomore year in high school. At the age of eleven, he became fascinated with the acting process. "One of the main reasons I got involved in acting is when I saw a play and it touched me so much. It opened my eyes," he explained to *Total TV.* "Even though I'd been watching movies prior to that and watching television as a child, something happened to me on that night. Every time I went to the movies after that, I looked at them differently than I know a lot of kids looked at them. Maybe I was more aware of what was happening in terms of the emotional journeys I was being taken on in terms of making me cry, making me think, making me laugh, making me wonder. Whatever the magic of being in movies or seeing a good television show did to me, I wanted to be part of that. I wanted to do that to other people."

He next attended Grandview Middle School and Mound West Tonka High School, where he participated in football, basketball, and baseball and was a member of the student council. From there he moved on to the University of Minnesota and Moorhead State, where he had a double major of marketing and advertising. He not only played football there but began appearing on stage as well. He dropped out of school in his senior year to pursue acting full time.

He began at age twenty-one with a stint at Kim Dawson's modeling agency and an actors/theater group in Dallas. Three years later he went to Europe, residing first in Milan, and then Munich, and finally moving to Sydney, Australia. He appeared in community theater and six commercials, among them a beer spot. "Yes," he sighed, "I did beer ads, but as a starving actor you do what you can to work, too. I didn't want to slut myself for it. I worked very well commercially, and commercials opened the door for me to where I am today. And I didn't have to bartend or do all those things most actors have to do. I was very fortunate."

He also decided to stay on in Australia for a while and live out a childhood fantasy. "I've always wanted to go to Australia," he admitted. "I wrote a book report about it when I was in fourth grade, on what country do you want to visit the most? It was one of those geography classes, and I wrote about Australia. I'd always been interested in it. I saw all those *National Geographic* specials. I went down there to shoot a commercial and stayed for six months. I did commercials and traveled around the Great Barrier Reef. I absolutely love it down there."

He managed a two-line debut on a 1983 episode of *Dallas* but didn't move to Los Angeles until 1986. Once there, he did manage to score some commercial work, pitching products such as Diet Coke and Lexus. Additionally, there were guest-starring stints in shows such as Angela Lansbury's *Murder, She Wrote;* Cybill Shepard's *Cybill;* and Stephen J. Cannell's *The Commish.* He also starred in the respective NBC and Fox pilots, *Critical Condition* and *Aspen.*

Still, true success eluded him despite his perseverance. He tested for the aforementioned roles of Fox Mulder and John Kelly on, respectively, *The X-Files* and Steven Bochco's *NYPD Blue.* He also tested for, and apparently was close to getting signed to, *Lois & Clark: The New Adventures of Superman* in the dual role of Clark Kent and Superman, a role that ultimately went to Dean Cain. What was especially frustrating in the latter instance was the fact that his agent told him he had the part and then, twenty-four hours later, informed him of the casting of Cain.

"They say you're supposed to develop a thick skin," he told journalist Scott Barwick. "You know what? We're actors, and actors deal with their emotions. So, yeah, you take it personally. You get upset about it. For me, it's another trip to the gym. You work out and get it out of your system. So I got over it. And, really, when it comes down to it, Dean was right for the part anyway. He's a much better Superman than I would be. And everything worked out the way it was supposed to."

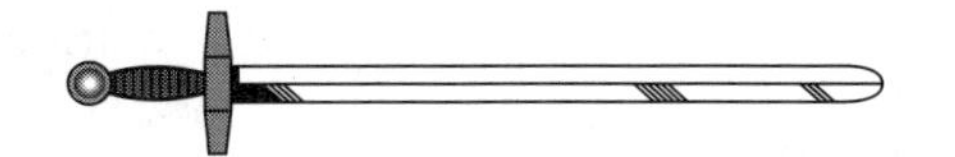

"They wanted to take [Hercules] out of the element of Greece and out of the toga. I felt it had this Last of the Mohicans meets Robin Hood quality to it."
—Kevin Sorbo

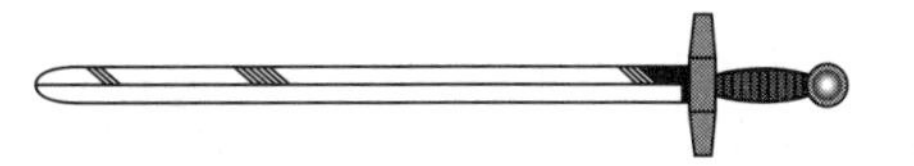

Indeed. In 1993, Sorbo's life changed forever when producers Robert Tapert and Sam Raimi—having been turned down by *Rocky IV*'s Dolph Lungren—signed him up as Hercules in a series of Universal TV movies that made up the studio's syndicated "Action Pack," which included *Midnight Run, Smokey and the Bandit, Vanishing Son,* and William Shatner's *TekWar.*

"When I got the script I kind of reacted the way that everybody else did," he explained. "There was a laughable quality about it. You know, 'Oh, *please*, what *is* this?' I read the first script, then the second, and finally the third and said, 'You know what? This is actually pretty cool.' Sam Raimi and Rob Tapert were looking for a completely different way to look at what Hercules is. They wanted to take him out of the element of Greece and out of the toga. I felt it had this *Last of the Mohicans* meets Robin Hood quality to it. The appeal of it for me was the humor—the fight scenes were over the top with almost that *Naked Gun* quality to them. There are dramatic moments, there are light moments, the special effects . . . so many different things that are appealing about the show."

The transformation of the movies into a series was actually not surprising to him. "While we were shooting the third movie," he related, "I was sitting on the set one day and I said, 'You know, this thing is going to be made into a series. I have a feeling this is going to become a series.' I go in there a couple of days later and they said, 'What have you heard?' 'I haven't heard. It's just a gut feeling.' Well, about six weeks later the studio called and said, 'We want to pick it up for a season, maybe do a series out of it.' The contract talks started happening. I just saw the appeal in terms of what the show is. There are dramatic beats, comedic beats, special effects. The fight sequences are done with sort of a wink. The large appeal of the show is that we don't take ourselves too seriously, and the audience knows it. We bring the audience in for the ride with us. And I think they really enjoy that. To tell you the truth, when we started, the idea was to appeal to teenage kids and youngsters, but I get grandmothers writing to me."

He admits to getting pleasure out of the fact that he is following in the long tradition of Steve Reeves (who portrayed Hercules on film nearly three decades earlier), Arnold Schwarzenegger, and Lou Ferrigno, all of whom have played the Greek before him. "Physically," he mused, "they're different Herculeses. I mean, Arnold and Lou are the bodybuilders, and I think their Hercs are far more serious and far more one-dimensional in a way. I think this Hercules is far more human. I love him. I think his appeal lies in the fact that he isn't Superman. He can get hurt, he can bleed, and yet he's willing to put his life on the line for other people. He is more accessible, I think, to people, and I think that's one of the reasons why the show is successful, because people, even though they can't relate to the fact that he's this half-god–strongest-man thing, whatever he's got going, I think he's more vulnerable. He'll make mistakes. He'll make fun of himself. He'll get beat up."

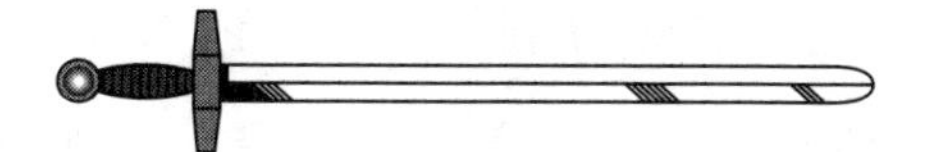

"I believe in my abilities. I believe I can play a black pregnant woman, so leave me alone."

—Kevin Sorbo

"If people want to pigeonhole me, that's just one more thing you've got to prove to people. I believe in my abilities. I believe I can play a black pregnant woman, so leave me alone."

—Kevin Sorbo

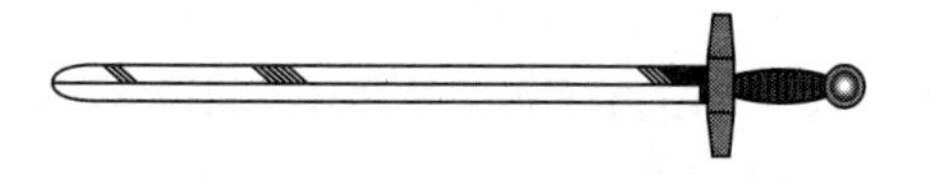

Another appeal for him about the character is the basic morality he's equipped with, which ties in fairly well with Sorbo's rather strict Lutheran upbringing.

"My parents were very religious, but it wasn't beat into you or you'll burn in hell forever," he told *Spectrum* magazine. "I certainly have my beliefs, and I carry them with me. I probably don't practice them as I should. I certainly don't preach them to people. I go nuts with that Bible-banging sort of mentality. It's up to the individual; I don't think you should have to beat people on the head with that. To me, it certainly is a big draw with the show. . . . And one of the big draws for me is the fact that we do have that moral message in there. I think it is important. I get letters from schools and hospitals and churches. Mythology is on this huge revival now. I'm not ashamed to say I think the show has a big part in that."

Although *Hercules: The Legendary Journeys* was pretty much attacked by the nation's television critics when the series started, the audience really latched on to it, resulting in a rapid, steady rise in its ratings. First, the show passed *Baywatch,* but, more shockingly, it was the first syndicated series to surpass *Star Trek: Deep Space Nine.*

"I guess we came out of the gate pretty strong, and the ratings slowly started hitching up every month where we were beating *Baywatch* and then *Star Trek.* I realized pretty early on that we had something special here," Sorbo explained. "In fact, I think it motivated us, especially [co-star] Michael Hurst and I to make the show the best it could be. You do reach a burnout stage because you're battling different things all the time in terms of story lines and everything else. You just want to make it good because the final product is you up there. You *want* to make it

Like Robin Is to Batman, Iolaus Is to Hercules

Trying to imagine Hercules without Iolaus, is like trying to picture Batman without Robin, the Lone Ranger without Tonto, or more importantly peanut butter without jelly. It might work, but it simply wouldn't taste as good.

Since the very first *Hercules* TV movie, Michael Hurst has portrayed Herc's best friend and partner in heroics, Iolaus. The actor describes the character as "fiercely loyal, brave, and headstrong." This makes sense when one realizes that Iolaus often acts on impulse, throwing himself against seemingly impossibly odds, perhaps forgetting the fact that it is Hercules—not he—who is a demigod. Iolaus also manages to supply the series with much of its humor.

"I think I remind Hercules of what it's like to be human all the time," Hurst told *Starburst* magazine. "I'm always the first one who wants to get into the action, and very often I'm the first one to say, 'Help!'"

At the age of thirty-nine, Hurst has become one of New Zealand's top actors and directors. Indeed, he helmed the third-season *Hercules* episode "Mercenary," the fourth season's " ... And Fancy Free," and the *Xena* episode "A Day in the Life."

Born in Lancashire, England, the actor moved to Christchurch, New Zealand, with his family when he was seven. During high school he began his path to an acting and directing career, performing those functions for school plays. In 1979, at the age of twenty-one, Hurst moved to Auckland to join Theatre Corporate. He was there for seven years, and his roles ranged from Scrooge in Dickens' *A Christmas Carol* to Shakes-

(continued)

good. It's hard to be up every single day, every single week, every single scene. Sometimes I walk through and I get mad at myself afterwards."

Not making things much easier is the sheer physicality of the role and the series, which requires that he stay in perfect shape or suffer the consequences.

"At times," he admitted, "the physical part is difficult because there are lots of stunts and fights and your body

peare's *Macbeth,* Mozart in *Amadeus,* and King Herod in *Jesus Christ Superstar* at the Mercury Theater in Auckland.

In 1987, Hurst became the first New Zealand actor to be contracted to Australia, where he played D'Artagnan in the Melbourne Theatre Company's production of *The Three Musketeers.* Besides acting, Hurst also handled fighting and fencing choreography. A year later, he was back in New Zealand and starring in stage productions of *South Pacific, Ladies Night, The Cherry Orchard,* and again *The Three Musketeers.* In 1989, he followed with a directing stint of *King Lear* at the Auckland University Summer Shakespeare Festival, then it was back to Australia for a starring role in *Romeo and Juliet.*

With the 1990s came a variety of starring stage roles, including *The Three Penny Opera, Richard III, Cabaret,* and *Hamlet* and the directorial efforts *The Merchant of Venice, Lysistrata, Macbeth, Cabaret, Romeo and Juliet, Hamlet,* and *Othello.*

As Patrick Stewart, best known as *Star Trek: The Next Generation*'s Captain Jean Luc Picard, has often stated, more people have probably seen him in a single episode of *Trek* than in all his extensive stage work combined. The same can undoubtedly be said about Michael Hurst, who seems proud of both his role and *Hercules* as a whole.

"One thing that's interesting is that I do an awful lot of Shakespeare," he told journalist Joe Nazzaro, "and although what we say in *Hercules* isn't exactly Shakespeare, the heroic stance that we often take is very similar to playing a great Shakespearean role. I'm no stranger to running around with swords and doing sword fights and great physical, athletic things because it's only a sidestep from the kind of work I've been doing in the past."

just gets worn out. You just have to go to the gym. Ninety minutes and *every* day. I like combinations of activity; I'll lift weights at the gym, run, swim, play basketball. I do love working out, but it's hard not to get bored. That's why I cross-train—so I don't end up doing the same thing all the time. I have a body that, if you apply yourself, you could potentially achieve what I look like. I'm an everyday man with a physique anybody could acquire.

"The problem is that I really don't have much of a personal life. I have no time for it. Zero. Can't go to the movies or dinner. By the time I leave the house, by the time I'm done on the set, thirteen hours average, then you go straight to the gym. Then I come back home and you shower and then you eat, then you look at the next eight pages that you've got to memorize for the next day. Then you go to bed. During the week, you really live for the show.

"It's not like being a football player, but there is that day-in-and-day-out grind of getting up and doing the fights," he added. "I've probably done more than three hundred fights in the show to date. Of course, Michael Hurst and I also work with a fantastic stunt team. They do the really dangerous things. Since there's no time to rehearse because of our hectic schedule, we learn the fights on the day we do them. As far as learning my lines, I have to study at night when I get home from shooting, in my car, in my makeup trailer, during lunch, and whenever else I can grab a few minutes.

"And there have been some real-life injuries. The worst was from Michael Hurst himself, as Iolaus. He hit me with his sword big time in the back of the head. It was totally his fault. He knew it, and I let him know I wasn't too happy about it. Thank God he hit me with the side of the sword because if he had hit me on the blade side, the doctor would've popped my skull open. He hit me in the side and cut a three-inch gash, and it took nine stitches to close. We had words the next day, Michael and I, because we had to stay friends, so we had to address it. But if I would have turned my face into that, that would have been it for my career, basically. Another time, I got hit by a guy that weighed four hundred pounds. He was a seven-time New Zealand weightlifting champion. Michael was an accident. This guy *wanted* to hit me. He didn't like the fact that I got to beat him up. I'm like, 'Dude, it's a TV show. Get your own show.' And he clocked me; he hit me so hard he broke two of my teeth. I was *not* happy."

The success of *Hercules* was so amazing that the producers of the show created a spin-off, starring Lucy Lawless as Xena, the Warrior Princess. Introduced on *The Legendary Journeys,* the Xena character was featured in a variety of episodes in which she essentially went through a transformation from evil to good. The spin-off has actually grown even *more* popular than its progenitor. Further spin-offs include the made-for-video *Young Hercules* and the animated *Hercules & Xena: The Battle for Mount Olympus.*

The success of *Xena* has resulted in numerous questions from fans of the series—some with way too much time on their hands—who have often debated who would win a battle between the two characters. Although such a hypothetical question seems ludicrous on the surface (reminding one of the moment in *Stand By Me* when that film's young performers ponder whether Mighty Mouse could take Superman in a fight), Sorbo actually looks at it quite seriously. Yes, he handles the question adeptly, but one can easily sense the frustration in the actor in terms of the lack of consistency the series has demonstrated regarding the true strength of the son of Zeus.

Sorbo told *Total TV,* "It sounds like I'm being nit-picky, jealous, or petty or something, but the thing is, Hercules was a real mythological character. Xena is totally fabricated, made up. The thing is, Hercules was the strongest person in the world. Period. . . . This is one of my fights with the writers. I get that question a lot from fans. Is she a god, too? You guys have to draw the line. They even ask about Iolaus because Iolaus beats up guys easier than I do. [Then,] when I hit guys, they fly a hundred yards. I said, 'You guys have to watch that. There's a fine line in there to make it that way.' There's got to be a reason why you make it that way. I think that part of the appeal of Hercules is that as affable as he is, as funny as he can be, and as human as he

"We get snubbed left and right. They can bypass me for best actor . . . but to bypass our set designers, the cinematography, our special effects—there is no show on TV that looks this good."

—Kevin Sorbo

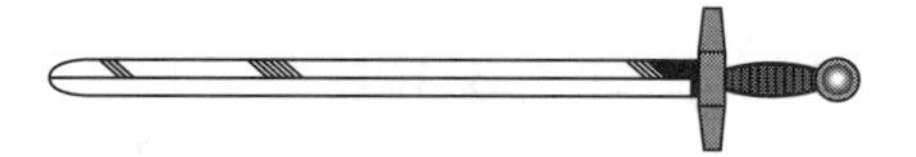

can be, part of the appeal to the watcher is that he still has this thing that we don't have. That's what's fun for me to play. As a kid growing up, I used to always fantasize about being indestructible, that I could go in and take care of the bad guys and save the world. The fight I had before Xena became a good girl . . . I said, 'Guys, she's a kung fu artist and can flip around and do all this stuff. Still, if I got a hold of her, I could snap her like a twig.' And they go, 'Well, you don't want to do that because you have to play it like you're trying to defend yourself because you don't want to hurt her.' But the way the fight is set up, it looks like it's pretty even or that she's beating me up. So I always had problems with that, but I'm more than happy to say that, in reality, Lucy really could beat me up.

"I get crazy with the inconsistency in the way they write his strength," he elaborated to *TV Guide*. "Why in one show do I have trouble fighting one guy who's a mortal, and in another show twenty guys come up to me and I flip them around like nothing? Why can Xena and Iolaus do as much, sometimes more, than I do? And they're mortals! Don't forget the fact that Hercules is a half-god. For somebody to come up behind me and hit me in the head with the butt end of a sword and I get knocked out—I'll argue that. Certainly I think it bothers the fans. The fans aren't stupid. Don't treat them that way. Sometimes we paint these pictures that are *so* connect-the-dots. I don't like that."

Another thing he doesn't like is the fact that, despite the success surrounding the series, there are certain frustrations stemming from the fact that the show airs in syndication as opposed to on one of the networks.

"Syndicated shows aren't what they were ten or fifteen years ago," Sorbo continues. "Hats off to *Star Trek: The Next Generation* for really opening the doors for shows like this to be made again. People were laughing at this show in the beginning, but now there are nothing but rip-offs of it. We've got the *Xena* spin-off, *Tarzan, Robin Hood, Sinbad, Conan.* All of these shows are trying to clone this show, and that, to me, is very flattering. What makes me mad are the Emmy nominations. We get snubbed left and right. They can bypass me for best actor—that's fine because I don't even know what category you put this show in anyway. But to bypass our set designers, the cinematography, our special effects—there is no show on TV that looks this good."

That being said, Sorbo emphasized that the only real drawback to starring in *Hercules*—more so than the long hours or the physical pressures—is the fact that the show shoots in New Zealand, pulling him away from America and his friends and family.

"It is certainly a cause of great frustration," he noted. "I am grateful for what the show has done for me, but at the same time I am not able to take advantage of the wonderful opportunities that are presented to me because of where I am at. That's life. I really do miss things like watching football games, going to hockey games, basketball. I miss the California weather. I miss Mexican food. And, of course, I miss my friends and family. I miss movies. It sounds bad, like I'm bashing New Zealand. It's gorgeous country, but they're lucky if they get fifty days of sun in a year. The homesickness thing really was tough for the first year and a half. It took me about that long to say, 'This is home.' I keep a place in Nevada, but I never get to use it. I don't know what I call home anymore. I still feel like I'm living out of a suitcase in a way. That's part of the thing that I get nuts about, too."

To nullify the negatives, Sorbo has been, as noted above, attempting to carve out a movie career for himself. Unfortunately, he hasn't been that lucky. His intended second film, *Black Dog,* in which he was to play an ex-con who's set up by the mob to drive a truck filled with illegal weapons, fell through because of a shoulder aneurysm. Plus, prior to that, *Kull* failed to ignite the box office charts and proved once again that success on the small screen does not necessarily translate to the big one. Still, for Sorbo the appeal of playing Kull was in the differences between he and Hercules and the character's more human side in terms of his darker emotions. Kull is someone from the "wrong side of the tracks," and he's an outcast of sorts from his people, who claim that he is not one of their own.

"It's the age-old story of racism, and I love the story of the underdog," he noted. "It was a chance to try on a different mask. Hercules is not a buffoon, but he's a guy that does make fun of himself and stumbles and makes mistakes. He tries to teach by example, but he learns by mistake as well. Kull is just more of a pitbull. He's a guy who's relentless and has more of an edge, which makes it more interesting to play than something like Hercules, where probably half of the character is me. It's not like it's a big stretch for me to play him. There are many actors on television shows right now who were in my acting class. These guys make a living off their personality, and most actors do in a way. Take someone like Tim Allen from *Home Improvement*—that's *him.* But he's likable, and it's a good show. It's also why you watch Jack Nicholson in a movie—you're watching to see Jack."

Which, Sorbo emphasizes, is by no means meant to disrespect the Greek guy, whose televised adventures have been renewed to March of the year 2000, though Sorbo's contract expires a year earlier.

"Do I want to keep doing it?" he asked rhetorically. "Today, yes. Tomorrow? I don't know. But I still enjoy the show, I still enjoy the people I work with. I have one complaint: I miss America. Otherwise we've got a great crew, and as long as the writing stays fun and inventive, I want to keep going. And the fourth season is off to a great start. I think [we've] got a Hercules classic in this season's premiere called 'Beanstalks and Bad Eggs.' The story is basically a hilarious reworking of 'Jack and the Beanstalk' in which Hercules and Autolycus, played by our good friend Bruce Campbell, climb a beanstalk to save a kidnapped woman and have to deal with an evil giant, who ends up being the twin brother of [recurring character] Typhon. The show is a hoot. We're up there bouncing around in the clouds, and we're chasing after Harpies, which, in the mythological world, are pretty nasty little critters. In the episode called '. . . And Fancy Free,' I wind up ballroom dancing in a sort of matador outfit. I really got a kick out of that. There's a parallel-universe episode in which I get to play both Hercules and a guy known as The Sovereign, who's a really nasty piece of work. Now that we're in our fourth season, Rob Tapert and the writers are really stirring things up. It continues to be an interesting mix of both comedy and drama. I think the biggest challenge is keeping the show fresh for ourselves so we can continue to make it exciting for the audience. It's important for me as an actor to keep expanding the dimensions of my character, so I appreciate it when the writers throw new things our way.

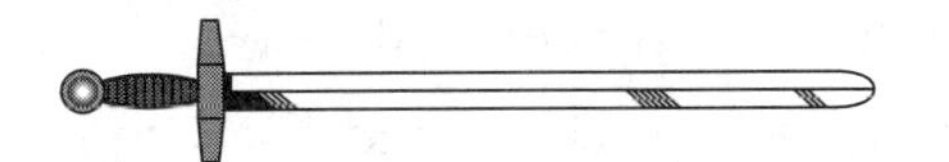

"My guess is that twenty years from now, college kids who aren't even born yet will be watching this show in reruns, and I'll be sitting somewhere with a big beer belly signing autographs."

—Kevin Sorbo

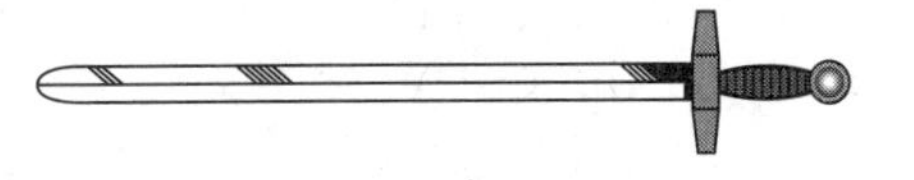

"My guess," he elaborated, "is that twenty years from now, college kids who aren't even born yet will be watching this show in reruns, and I'll be sitting somewhere with a big beer belly signing autographs. In the last season of the series maybe I'll be sitting in a rocking chair, people will come over and say, 'Hey, help us Hercules,' and I'll be like, 'F--- off.' Then we can do a bunch of bottle shows where I'll say, 'Remember when we beat that hydra to hell?' and we'll rely on flashbacks and do the show in like two days. We'll call it *Herc: The Old Years.*"

Turning more serious, Sorbo does note with interest the impact the series has had on the Internet as well as the show's fan base. He's still surprised at its ever-increasing popularity.

"The show, for better or for worse, is still growing," he says. "My negative feeling about syndication is that if we were on a network at the same time every week, our ratings would be double what they are in syndication. Syndication [in the states] is tough because you're on different stations at different times in every city across the country. Yet now we're in sixty-one countries, and that's constantly expanding. The audience isn't dropping off at all, and a lot of it is word of mouth. A lot of letters I get from fans are like, 'I heard about his show over the last two years, and people have told me to watch it. I flipped it on and watched it and said, "That's okay." Then I watched it a week later, and now I get the show and it's a trip.' That's how we built our fan base to the point it is.

"The truth is," Sorbo added, "that in New Zealand people pretty much leave me alone. I can cruise around and do my own thing. It's when I come back to the States and even in Europe that I realize how big *Hercules* has become. I recently went to the grand opening of Planet Hollywood in Key West, and I was blown away by the outpouring of fans who were screaming as I walked into the place—many of them even knew my real name! But, believe me, I don't say to myself, 'Boy, do I deserve this.' It's overwhelming. I think all of this will hit me ten years from now. It's wonderful, but quite surreal.

"The Internet is just as amazing," he continued. "I don't pop in there all the time, but I do occasionally, and I'm blown away by all the Web pages.

Again, surreal is the only word I can come up with. Then you're walking through the stores and you see your photo on boxes of toys and underwear and the realization is, 'Wow, I'm the Adam West of my generation.' I look at it that way because if I had met Adam West when I was seven years old, I would have freaked out. When little kids walk on the set or I'm walking down the street and they're having little heart attacks, you want to say, 'Relax, it's just a TV show,' but to them it isn't."

HERCULES: THE LEGENDARY JOURNEYS

Series Overview

IF IT WASN'T FOR THE FUTURE, THE ANCIENT PAST OF *HERCULES: THE Legendary Journeys* would probably never have existed.

More accurately, if not for the phenomenal syndicated success of Paramount Pictures' *Star Trek: The Next Generation,* no one would have attempted to tap into what was, until that time, a source of very little profit. Indeed, prior to the 1987 premiere of *Next Generation,* syndication—a process by which independent stations around the country agree to air a television series, therefore allowing a studio to bypass the networks—was deemed a dumping ground for inferior, low-budget products.

Having failed to strike a deal with the networks on an unproven commodity, despite the worldwide success of the original *Star Trek,* Paramount dove completely into syndication, pouring the kind of money and production value into the series that, until that point, had been seen only on the "big three" networks: ABC, NBC, and CBS. It was a calculated risk, but one that paid off handsomely as the show's ratings, and therefore profits, rose briskly, driving home more than ever the notion of *Trek* as phenomenon. Others jealously watching the profits pouring into Paramount attempted to jump on the bandwagon, with Warner Brothers being the first to do so by offering *Time Trax, Kung Fu: The Legend Continues,* and *Babylon 5,* with only the latter developing any kind of serious following.

Universal also began seeking a piece of the action. One of the most powerful providers to the medium, the studio grew determined to prove that it could rule syndication in much the same way that it would periodically rule primetime. To this end, it decided to produce a series of television movies under the umbrella title "Action Pack," based loosely on NBC's classic mystery wheel anthology that included *Columbo, McCloud,* and *McMillan and Wife.* In this case, the TV movies consisted of *Smokey and the Bandit* and *Midnight Run,* which were based on theatrical films of the same name and faded much quicker than the others. Additionally, there was *Vanishing Son,* a moderate hit dealing with two Asian brothers, each existing on opposite sides of the law. Then there was William Shatner's *TekWar,* a well-produced science fiction effort taking place a few years in the future and dealing with a former cop's battle to stop addiction to a virtual reality, drug-like technology. Four *TekWar* films were produced, followed by a single season series.

No doubt the most unexpected surprise of the "Action Pack" was something called *Hercules: The Legendary Journeys,* a hip, tongue-in-cheek production that mixed humor, spectacle, and state-of-the-art special effects. In many ways, the production modernized the mythological hero (a wicked sense of humor replaced the togas) and made him palatable for modern audiences. At the same time, it managed to reach back into our collective memories by miraculously recapturing the magic of Ray Harryhausen-like special effects that were the hallmarks of such films as *The Seven Voyages of Sinbad, Jason and the Argonauts,* and *Sinbad and the Eye of the Tiger.* The effects made them more realistic, thanks to a combination of stop motion and CGI. There's no denying that Hercules' battles with various hydras, sea serpents, cyclopes, and centaurs are, for the most part, completely convincing and unlike anything else currently on the air, all thanks to the efforts of F/X guru Kevin O'Neill and Flat Earth Productions.

Everyman Kevin Sorbo effortlessly stepped into the sandals first worn by Steve Reeves in a bunch of cheesy Italian films and became part of a formula that won audiences the world over. Five TV movies were produced, followed by a subsequent series that at present is in the midst of its fourth season and that amazingly has already been renewed through the year 2000.

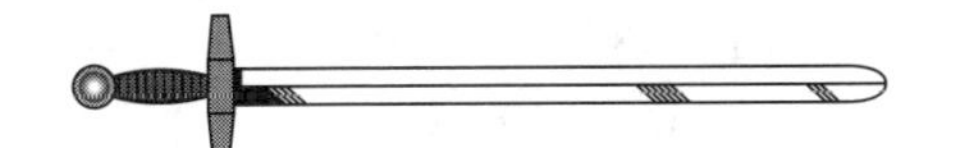

"I think we filled a void. We wanted to do a Butch Cassidy and the Sundance Kid–style version of Hercules with monsters and special effects and contemporary dialogue, and it worked."

—Executive Producer Robert Tapert

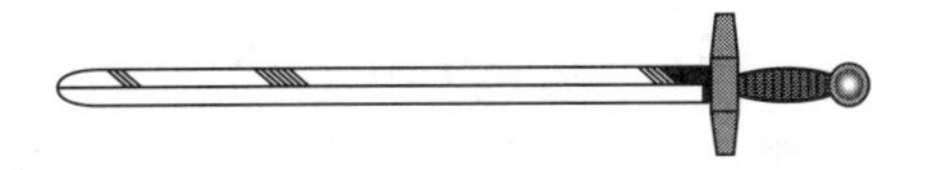

Behind *Hercules,* which films in New Zealand, is the producing team of Sam Raimi and Robert Tapert, whose unique style of filmmaking had endeared them to audiences in such films as the *Evil Dead* trilogy, *Darkman, Hard Target, The Quick and the Dead,* and *Timecop* as well as such television series as *American Gothic* and *M.A.N.T.I.S.* Their trademark, for the most part, was mixing excitement with humor, and it was a formula that had obviously come together perfectly on *Hercules,* which was created by writer Christian Williams.

Adding to the show's success is a variety of subsidiary characters who play off of Hercules and, in some cases, provide a great deal of humor, among them Michael Hurst as Herc's best friend and sidekick, Iolaus; Bruce Campbell (star of the *Evil Dead* films) as Autolycus, the so-called King of Thieves; Kevin Smith as Ares, the god of war; Alexandra Tydings as the goddess of love, Aphrodite; and Robert Trebor as Salmoneus, best described as the world's first traveling salesman.

"When Universal asked us to do *Hercules*," Robert Tapert told the press, "we said we could never beat *Star Trek,* but we always had our eyes on doing better than *Baywatch.* We figured that if we just told good stories and kept the action up, we could get viewers. I think we filled a void. We wanted to do a Butch Cassidy and the Sundance Kid–style version of Hercules with monsters and special effects and contemporary dialogue, and it worked. Instead of togas and cyclopes, we got a good-looking quarterback, the sort of guy you'd like to have in your living room every week. There was nothing like it on TV, and viewers found us right away."

When Universal decided to spin the films off into a weekly series, both Raimi and Tapert realized that they would have to find someone to run the show's writing staff who knew how to work in that medium, which was quite different from two-hour movies of the week. They found their man in John Schulian, a journalist-turned-scriptwriter whose credits include *Slap Maxwell, Wiseguy,* and *Midnight Caller.* For two and a half seasons, Schulian was the creative guiding force behind the series along with Tapert, setting the tenor and largely responsible for its appeal.

"Never in my wildest dreams did I ever picture myself doing *Hercules,*" says Schulian candidly. "I'm not saying that I looked down on it, it just wasn't anything that I aspired to. My idea when I came out to Los Angeles was to do Bochcoesque-type shows. But here I was, and I was intrigued by it. They sent me a couple of the two-hour movies, and I automatically liked Kevin Sorbo, the star of the show. I thought he was a big, good-looking guy who wasn't built like a municipal statue. He had a nice self-effacing quality. He was just very likable in that Tom Selleck way, a guy who's just made to be a TV star. People are willing to invite him into their home."

According to Schulian, when Christian Williams created *Hercules,* he was reportedly hoping for a series that would appeal to motorcycle gangs as well as college professors. "My goals weren't quite that lofty," laughs Schulian. "I thought it should be a show that kids could watch and adults would see the humor in. It sort of works on two levels, and I knew we were on to something when my assistant told me that her sister, who was a student at Berkeley, had reported that the fraternity houses were not going out on Saturday nights until after they'd watched *Hercules.* That is *exactly* the kind of thing we wanted—that it would be in whatever bizarre way a kind of hip show. And I don't know what makes things hip. I'm the least hip guy in the world. What we did, as hard as it may be to believe, is that we did not write these shows to be campy, they simply are. We wrote these things as straight down the middle. Granted we put gags and jokes in them, but we didn't go overboard, appealing to the automatic campiness that a project like this has. I take my work seriously, but I try not to take myself seriously, and in some ways it's a reflection of that."

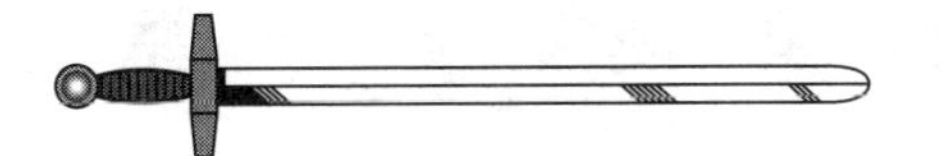

"I don't think anything is simple in this business, no matter what kind of show you're doing. Whether you're doing lawyers or super heroes, it still requires a certain amount of thought and effort."
—Co-executive Producer John Schulian

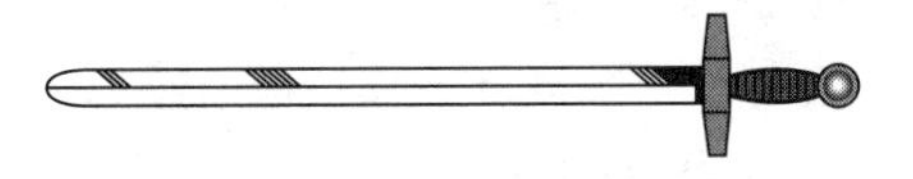

As he explains it, Schulian's take on the series was that it was a western that just happened to take place in the ancient past.

"I had never written mythology," he says, "but I had certainly seen a lot of western movies, and I know about single protagonists or single-hero-type shows. Hercules was that good man who goes into that wild and wooly town and cleans it up every week. I could understand that, and they

Production and Special Effects Terminology

DAILIES: Everyone has the impression that Hollywood is this magical place. While the end result may, indeed, reflect this conception, the day to day process would put just about anyone not in the biz right to sleep. At the end of a day's worth of shooting—in which the same scene is often shot over and over again ad nauseum—the show's creative staff will gather to look at the footage of that day's work, known as Dailies. There they will pick the best takes and angles and start the blueprint of how the show will ultimately be cut together.

CGI: No, it's not a branch of the government. CGI is short for Computer Generated Images, and it is here to stay. All of the cool additions that George Lucas made to the recent "special edition" *Star Wars* trilogy, Steven Spielberg's multitude of dinosaurs from *Jurassic Park* and *The Lost World*, and many of the effects from *Hercules: The Legendary Journeys* owe their very existence to the power of the computer. It is difficult to remember filmmaking without them.

THE BLACK TOWER: Not to be confused with Stephen King's *The Dark Tower* book series, the "Black Tower," as it has been known for decades, is the foreboding office building on the Universal lot in which all of the studio's executives work and where plans for world domination are hatched (okay, maybe the last point is a bit of an exaggeration. Then again. . . .).

STORYBOARDS: The late, great Alfred Hitchcock swore by them. Storyboards are, quite literally, a visual mapping out of difficult sequences to be created on film for motion pictures or television. They are an intricate part of an effects-heavy show like *Hercules* because they give the show's actors, directors, and special effects technicians guidelines on how to stage the action so that the effects can be seamlessly inserted later.

FIRST & SECOND UNITS: Relatively speaking, first unit photography is the easier aspect of production. It is during this period where the cast delivers their dialogue and enters and exits action sequences. Second unit photography, on the other hand, usually consists of stunts, fights, and the action sequences in which stunt doubles do their thing and make the cast look so damn good.

LINE PRODUCER: This is the guy who basically makes it all happen. He's down in the trenches during the physical production of the show making sure that everything stays on time and on budget, and playing an integral role in guaranteeing that a show is the best that it can be.

CLIP & BOTTLE SHOWS: Generally speaking, if you're watching *Hercules* or any other type of show and are pretty blown away by the effects and action sequences as presented in several episodes, you can believe that the studio and the audience is going to have to pay for it somewhere down the line. Thus was born the so-called "clip" and "bottle" shows, in which the writers contrive some reason for one or two cast members to be confined to a very limited space so that they can reflect on their relationship and offer a wide multitude of flashbacks (i.e., filmclips) to earlier episodes. For the most part these episodes are ridiculous, dopey, and downright annoying. Nonetheless, they are a necessity of production.

STOP-MOTION ANIMATION: The special effects of *Hercules* will usually offer computer generated effects or creatures presented in stop motion animation. Stop motion is generally created when a special effects technician takes a model of a creature, shoots several frames of it, moves it ever so slightly, shoots several more frames, and continues the process again and again until, in the end, they have a creature that seems to be moving. For the best examples, check out the original *King Kong* and any film by Ray Harryhausen, including *Jason and the Argonauts*, *The Golden Voyage of Sinbad*, the *Beast From 20,000 Fathoms*, and so on.

agreed with my take on the show. I know that sounds easy, but it really isn't. I don't think anything is simple in this business, no matter what kind of show you're doing. Whether you're doing lawyers or superheroes, it still requires a certain amount of thought and effort. I understood what I wanted to do, although I'm not sure the writers that I wound up bringing in the

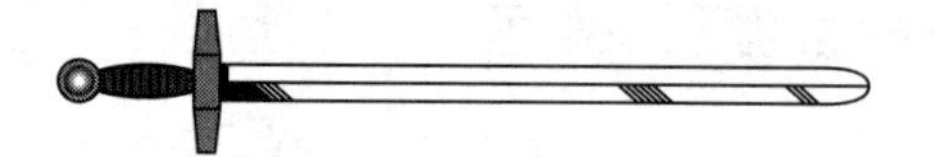

"[The episodes] had to be about good triumphing over evil, loyalty between people, about honoring a code—traditional things. They are little morality tales."
—Co-executive Producer John Schulian

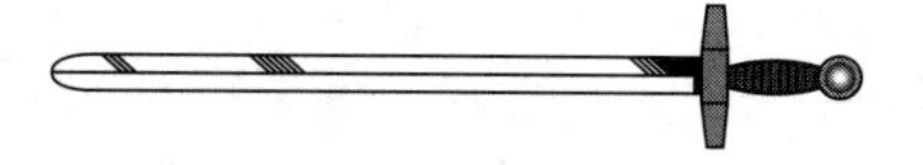

early going understood what I wanted. We wanted this show to have a sense of humor, to be contemporary without being stupid about it. In other words, nobody would say, 'Yo, dude.' The idea was to have action and to have heart, to be about *something.* I don't mean in any great cosmic way. I just mean they had to be about good triumphing over evil, loyalty between people, about honoring a code—traditional things. They are little morality tales. We wanted Hercules to be helping people and not just out killing people for fun. It wasn't much more complicated than that. I'm a big believer in keeping television series as simple as possible, that you work from that bare-bones structure and then you hang your canvas, paint it different ways, and it all comes out. But the basic stories are all very simple."

Robert Bielak joined *Hercules* first as a freelancer, then as supervising producer, and ultimately as co-executive producer. From the outset he enjoyed the show's mix, especially its humor. "The show was designed to have fun with itself," he notes. "That mix just worked for me, and I felt it might be fun to write, and if it's fun to write, it might be fun to act and direct, and people might watch."

And watch they did, resulting in the show's ratings climbing, ultimately passing the *Next Generation* spin-off, *Star*

Trek: Deep Space Nine. It proved itself to be one of the biggest phenomena in years and inspired the spin-off *Xena,* which has gone on to become an even bigger hit. Unfortunately, not everything has been pleasant on the making of the show, as evidenced by John Schulian's departure in the middle of the third season. For his part, Tapert explained Schulian's departure by noting, "There were a bunch of reasons—it was just time to move on."

According to Schulian, the reason he left the show was basically because he was forced out by Kevin Sorbo, who, according to what the writer had been told, had made his departure a contractual negotiation.

"Look, I thought Kevin was terrific as Hercules," Schulian explains. "But when you're in television, just as was the case when I was writing sports, you're in the business of building monsters: You try to create stars. Certainly that's the case in television. In newspapers and magazines you're writing about people, and the fact that you're writing about them and saying how wonderful they are, it transforms them into monsters. In television, you're trying to create stars, and when people become stars they react in different ways, not all of them good. So Kevin said something in an interview in the late and much-lamented *New York Newsday* where he took a shot at the writing on the show. It wasn't particularly flattering; basically trying to get across the idea that he had to save every script. I was overworked on that show. There was no staff, basically, and it just felt like a death march. So I was in no mood for that kind of crap. I wrote him a letter, and he called me from New Zealand, very flustered, saying he had been misquoted. I said, 'Kevin, I spent sixteen years in newspapers, and misquoted just isn't going to fly with me. If you don't like what I said, you can go to Rob and Sam and get me fired.' And he certainly has that power. He said, 'No, no, I would never do anything like that.' Well, the next year of course I became a sticking point in his contract negotiations. Look, I know who goes in a situation like that. I really felt I was an important cog in the show. Kevin is clearly the biggest cog, but when a television show or movie succeeds, it's because of a confluence of good things."

Bielak stepped into Schulian's position on the show and handled things well until it was decided that the show had to change direction in its fourth season if it was to stay on top. The new direction was not one that he felt very comfortable with. "When I first joined the show," he explains, "I felt that I really had a handle on it, that my scripts were fastballs down the middle. But now new writers have come in, and they're throwing the fastballs, and I found the change in direction difficult.

"After a while," he says, "everyone starts asking for something new, but you have to be careful because this is the franchise. You can't change that guy too much because this is who he is. He really is the Lone Ranger, and the Lone Ranger never had a qualm of conscience. He always did the right thing. We actually tried to get more into putting him on the horns of a dilemma. Unlike Xena, who's got a whole past you can go to, Hercules was always good, and he always will be. I also think that in the fourth season I was getting to a point where I would write a scene and say, 'Oh shit, I did that already.'"

Another problem was, interestingly enough, that the *Xena* series was actually draining potential story ideas. "We had the field to ourselves for the first thirteen episodes of *Hercules,*" says Bielak, who ultimately departed in the middle of the fourth season, "and then *Xena* got spun off, and that show was trying to find itself like we had been doing in the beginning. They weren't quite sure where the stories were going to slant. We already knew for ourselves, and it was still wide open for us. Toward the end of our second season and the end of *Xena*'s first, we started running into situations like, 'Well, we're doing that story on *Xena,* and we don't want to do it again.' That, coupled with the fact that the actors were starting to say, 'We've done this, can we do something a little different?' Even the writers were feeling the same way.

"Faced with the problem of repetition of ideas," he elaborates, "Rob Tapert said, 'Here's what's going to happen. We're in our fourth year, and they've already told me at the Tower that the numbers are going to start trickling down a little bit and eventually we'll be down to the hardcore audience because other people will lose interest if it's not fresh anymore. There's a certain group out there that will watch it forever, and there's another group that comes in because it's fresh, new, and different. When that wears off, they'll move on to something different.' So things have gotten harder and harder. It's a natural thing and how series evolve."

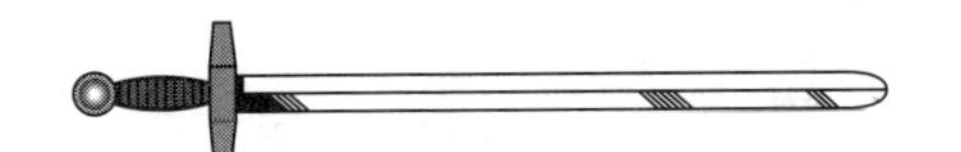

"The writing, while I would never say it was Shakespeare, served the purpose of the show. It established a sensibility and a voice for the show."
Co-executive Producer
John Schulian

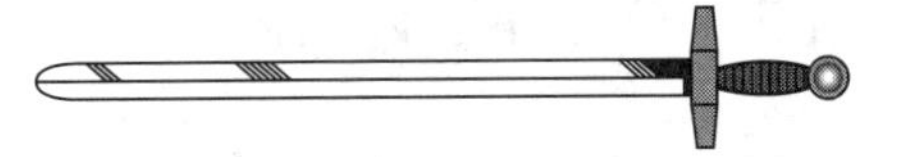

The bottom line is that despite the behind-the-scenes shake-ups, the audience seems to be enjoying the directions *Hercules* is traveling in its fourth year and shows absolutely no signs of abandoning it.

Despite no longer being involved with the show, Schulian offers what he feels is the reason that it has become so successful.

"Whether the creator of a successful television show is a genius like Steven Bochco or a lunkhead like me," he observes, "the bottom line is that you have caught lightning in a bottle. You're praying for a miracle. When you look at *Hercules,* which came out of nowhere, we had Kevin, we had a very good buddy co-star in Michael Hurst, we had New Zealand, which was a glorious place to shoot this show with lush landscape and, as a bonus, beautiful light, the kind of light that gave everything a golden cast, and it plays right into that mythological period

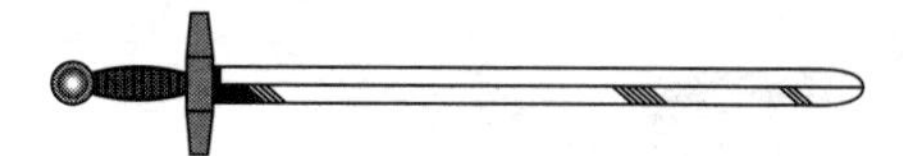

"After a while, everyone started asking for something new, but you have to be careful because this is the franchise.... He really is the Lone Ranger and the Lone Ranger never had a qualm of conscience. He always did the right thing."

—Co-executive Producer Robert Bielak

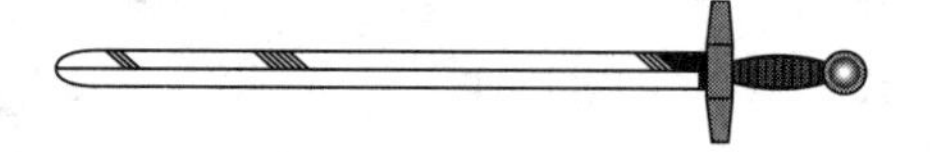

we're talking about. We had wonderful special effects, and the writing, while I would never say it was Shakespeare, served the purpose of the show. It established a sensibility and a voice for the show.

"One more reason that the show is so popular is because it filled a vacuum," he closes. "The networks have completely forgotten about doing this kind of show. All network dramas are about well-dressed people in handsomely appointed rooms, screaming at each other about angst, about misery. God knows I wrote for *Wiseguy,* I've worked that territory. I understand why writers want to do that, and certainly I hope that I get to go back and write miserable characters again. But the name of the business is entertainment, and I just think that the networks have forgotten about simply entertaining people. That's what we were trying to do on *Hercules*—taking people out of their world and away from divorces, drive-by shootings, and all the other things that make life in the nineties so much fun."

EPISODE GUIDE

THE LEGENDARY JOURNEYS OF HERCULES TV MOVIES

TVM #1: "Hercules and the Amazon Women"

Written by Julie Selbo, Andrew Dettman, and Daniel Truly

Directed by Bill L. Norton

Guest Starring Anthony Quinn (Zeus), Roma Downey (Hippolyta), Lloyd Scott (Pithus), Lucy Lawless (Lusia), and Jennifer Ludlam (Alcmene)

Infuriated by Zeus' infidelities with mortals, the goddess Hera has spent nearly all her time over the past few decades striking back in vengeance against Zeus' demigod son, Hercules. As the movie series commences, she picks the wedding of Hercules' best friend, Iolaus, as the setting for her latest attack by unleashing a hydra, a multiheaded giant snakelike creature.

This precipitates the arrival of Pithus, who is seeking the help of Hercules to protect his village of Dogernicia. This village has been under frequent attack, women always being the "treasure" taken. Both Hercules and Iolaus agree to help, temporarily postponing the wedding.

Investigating the situation, the duo are attacked by Amazons adorned in bizarre masks who kill Iolaus and take Hercules prisoner. Taken to their village, Hercules ultimately learns that the

Amazons—who feel they have been mistreated by the male gender and are seeking revenge—are secretly being pushed toward war with men by Hera. Given insight into his own actions and attitudes toward women—many of them shaped by Zeus' influence—by Hippolyta, Hercules goes through something of a change and tries to convince the men of the village that they too must change their ways to end the conflict with the Amazons.

At episode's end, Hercules approaches Zeus and asks him to use his powers as king of the gods to reverse what has taken place. A moment later, Hercules is back at Iolaus' wedding, and when Pithus arrives, he gives the man advice on how to approach the Amazons so that the attacks on the village will come to an end.

Behind the Scenes Doug Lefler, a storyboard artist and a second-unit director for Sam Raimi on *Army of Darkness,* performed both functions in the sequence of this film in which Hercules goes up against the hydra.

"They sent me to do second unit," he says, "because although the sequence was written into the script, we reworked it in the storyboarding process and really altered the visual aspects of it. Since I had storyboarded it, they thought that I was familiar enough with it that they sent me to New Zealand to do that sequence."

TVM #2: "Hercules and the Lost Kingdom"

Written by Christian Williams
Directed by Harley Cokeliss
Guest Starring Anthony Quinn (Zeus), Renee O'Connor (Deianeira), Robert Trebor (Waylin), Eric Close (Telmon), Barry Hill (King Ilus), Nathaniel Lees (Blue Monk), Onno Boelee (Gargan), and Elizabeth Hawthorne (Queen Omphale)

Something of a pattern becomes apparent when ninety-nine messengers from the missing kingdom of Troy have been killed, thanks to Hera's influence. Hercules becomes involved in the situation when messenger number one hundred dies in his arms and the demigod learns from his father, Zeus, that he must seek out the "One True Compass," which will lead him to the elusive Troy.

En route on his quest, he saves a woman named Deinareira from being sacrificed and finds himself unwittingly partnered with her in his search for the compass. They eventually find themselves in the presence of Queen Omphale of Lydia, who claims she can deliver the compass to him if Hercules will be her slave for a day. Equipped with the device, they are led to Troy, where Hercules must help the enslaved people rebel against the "Blue Cult of Hera."

Things aren't easy, naturally, as Hercules must suffer several trials, among them being swallowed by a sea serpent, which he must kill from the inside and then escape.

TVM #3: "Hercules and the Circle of Fire"

Written by Barry Pullman, Andrew Dettman, and Daniel Truly
Directed by Doug Lefler
Guest Starring Anthony Quinn (Zeus), Tawny Kitaen (Deianeira), Kevin Atkinson (Cheiron), Mark Ferguson (Prometheus), Mark Newham (Antaeus), Stephanie Barett (Phaedra), and Christopher Brougham (Janus)

Apparently still pissed off that Prometheus introduced fire to mortals, Hera—who seems to be suffering from a perennial case of PMS—removes the "Torch of Fire," thus plunging the Earth into darkness. Hercules takes it upon himself to right the situation and finds himself involved in a series of struggles to do so.

First off, he accidentally wounds a Satyr named Cheiron, a wound that he must find a way of mending or else the immortal creature will spend all eternity in pain. From there he meets up with an older, more mature Deianeira, who attempts to enlighten him to the fact that using his brain can be as effective as his brawn, a lesson seemingly lost on him when he nonetheless decimates Hera's temple out of anger for all he's been through at her hands. Adding to the "joy" of his quest is a battle with the giant Antaeus and the object of his obsession, which lie within Hera's Circle of Fire.

An interesting—and important—character moment occurs when Zeus offers his son the opportunity to join him on Mt. Olympus, but Hercules decides to remain on Earth to help humanity in its journey as a race and in its struggle against the wrath of the gods.

Behind the Scenes Explains storyboard artist and second-unit director-turned-director Doug Lefler, "I grew up on Ray Harryhausen films, and this was a chance to explore my childhood dreams and fantasies. It was perfect material for me to do. The *Hercules* two-hour movie I did was my first unit-directing debut. Even if it had been material I wasn't so in touch with, I still would have done it. It was just an added bonus that it was something I felt I could really have fun with. The scope of the project was not tough for me because before I became a director I was a storyboard artist for many years. Primarily what I did was take the complicated aspects of scenes and try to work out a way to do them. When I started actually doing the film, the effects and action were the things I felt comfortable with. Also, because when I was a second-unit director those were the things I was given to do. What scared me the first time was working with actors and trying to get a performance on film. *That* was frightening.

"That was also the part," he continues, "and as the years have gone by it has become more so—that was the most exciting and more enjoyable. It was all new territory, and it was one of the few aspects of directing that came a little more naturally to me. Everything else I learned how to do through a lot of sweat and effort. To tell you the truth, storyboarding was a great assistance to my directing, especially when I was starting out. Every one of these major action and special effects sequences I storyboarded and I submitted to the producers. Generally they looked at them and said, 'You're out of your mind, you're never going to pull this off in the time that you have.' It was interesting because we generally did put those sequences on film because I had done my homework, done the math, and I knew how many setups I could get each day. I had planned on a little more than that, thinking that I wanted to be more ambitious going in, and I always had some bits of the action sequences that I could drop if I had to. I always made sure I shot the beginning and the end of the sequence first and as much of the middle as I could. If I then had to condense it, I did, but I would cut from the middle, so this way I knew that, no matter what, I'd have a full sequence. The more time you had, the more you could elaborate on it and develop the sequence. It was a very exciting time, actually.

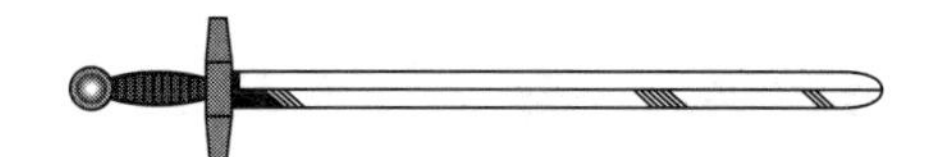

"I grew up on Ray Harryhausen films, and this was a chance to explore my childhood dreams and fantasies. It was perfect material for me to do."
—Director Doug Lefler

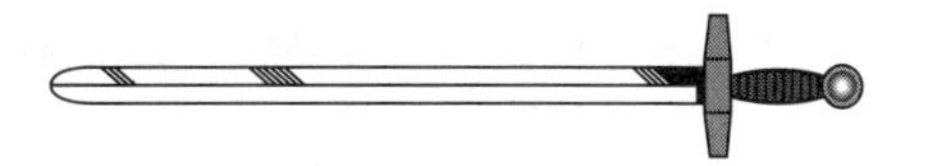

"One of the things that made the whole experience fun was that a lot of us were doing it for the first time. It was the first time that Renaissance had done something like it. I think in a lot of ways we did things that were bigger than people expected because we didn't know we couldn't do them. That made it very exciting, too. We were all feeling our way and helping each other out. I think it was about the best first directing assignment anyone could ask for.

"I really liked the film at the time. In retrospect, I find it is not as engrossing to me as some of the other ones. In retrospect, I think I probably enjoy watching *The Lost Kingdom* the best out of all of the TV movies, mainly because in *Circle of Fire* I was trying very hard to be clever. At the end of the day, I think the things that hold my attention the most are the ones that have an emotional core to them. I think that in *Circle of Fire* I was trying to be clever with the filmmaking and the storytelling, whereas the simple elements of storytelling are always stronger. It's always better to have a simple, strong structure and then elaborate on that rather than have complexity in the storytelling. In terms of how I feel about the overall experience, it was wonderful. To have a chance

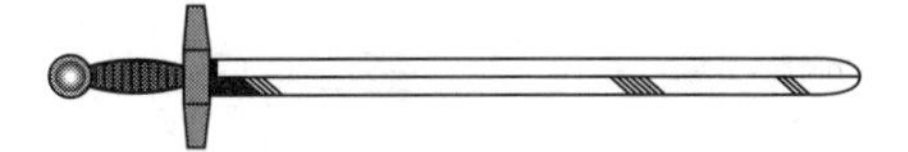

"One of the things we tried to do in Hercules is that we wanted the dialogue to be contemporary but didn't want anyone to say, 'Yo, dude.' That was the line that you could not cross."
—Co-executive Producer John Schulian

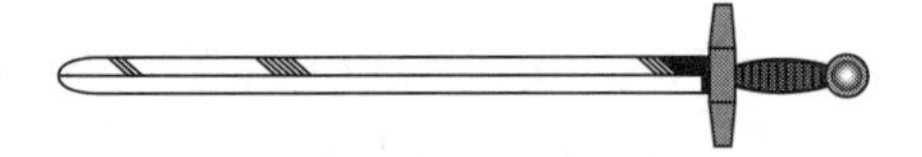

to work with Anthony Quinn on your directorial debut—what could be more incredible than that? One of the producers, when they were getting nervous about this being my first project, asked how I was going to get a performance out of Anthony Quinn. I said, 'Well, I'm going to point the camera at him.'

"One of the other things about that experience that was enjoyable to me was that it gave us the chance to explore some of the more old-fashioned methods of special effects. In high school, my parents gave me a book on the history of special effects technology. When I was given that book in the late '70s, every technique in it was out of date. I re-read many chapters of it before I went to New Zealand, and I consulted with some special effects story artists I'd met over the years. We explored many old-fashioned techniques. Forced perspective was among them. In this film we did a mirror shot, which is one of the oldest effects tricks in the book, about a hundred years old, and developed by a German cinematographer. Basically what you do is you have a full-size set and a miniature-size set, and you put a mirror up at a 45-degree angle to the camera. You scrape away the silver at the back of the mirror so it becomes a window that looks through to see the full-size set, and the top half of the mirror reflects the miniature. Like I said, it's one of the oldest techniques that's ever been done, but it works wonderfully. We used it for the sequence in *Circle of Fire* where Hercules goes to visit the Titan and he's sitting up on his throne and is frozen. It was all done in camera. We've done a lot of things with compositing miniatures and a lot of things where we've taken the miniature that was going to be photographed out and shot it in the same light as the plate was shot in. When you composite images, the most important thing is the lighting. By setting the model up at the same time and shooting it with the same sunlight and then pulling back and shooting the background plate, it allowed them to do composites in the computer that matched extremely well.

"So it was fun experimenting. We were taking bits of old techniques and bits of new techniques and combining them together, almost creating new forms of special effects. They were fun because you would do these old techniques, like set up a forced perspective shot where you'd set up a platform for the actor playing the giant closer to the camera. Then you'd dress the top of the platform so it would look like the ground in the distance. You'd look through the eyepiece, and it would match perfectly."

TVM #4: "Hercules in the Underworld"

Written by Andrew Dettman and Daniel Truly
Directed by Bill L. Norton
Guest Starring Anthony Quinn (Zeus), Tawny Kitaen (Deianeira), Timothy Balme (Lycastus), Michael Hurst (Charon), Mark Ferguson (Hades), Marlee Shelton (Iole), Cliff Curtis (Nessus), and Jorge Gonzales (Eryx)

Between TV movies, Hercules has married Deianeira and is the father of three children, but his declaration that he is determined to help humanity forces him to leave his family behind as he investigates a mysterious gas escaping from the Earth itself, which is killing members of a local village.

A woman named Iole—who turns out to be someone who lures men to their death—and a centaur named Nessus attempt to manipulate Hercules and lead him into one of Hera's traps at a fissure leading to Hades' underworld. No sooner has he descended than word reaches Deianeira that her husband has died. Filled with despair, she kills herself.

In the underworld, Hercules discovers that all . . . er . . . hell has broken loose as Cerberus, the guardian of the "gate," has broken free. Hades informs Herc of Deianeira's death and says that he will bring her back to life *if* the Greek can recapture Cerberus. Desperate, Hercules agrees to do so and, remembering Deianeira's lessons about brains over brawn, approaches the creature with kindness rather than force and manages to rechain it.

Surprisingly, Hades keeps his word, returning Deianeira to life and, as a bonus, stopping the deadly gas from entering the atmosphere.

TVM #5: "Hercules in the Maze of the Minotaur"

Written by Andrew Dettman and Daniel Truly
Directed by Josh Becker
Guest Starring Tawny Kitaen (Deianeira), Anthony Quinn (Zeus), Andrew Thurtill (Danion), Terry Bachelor (Trikonis), and Sydney Jackson (Darthus)

A man named Danion comes to Hercules and Iolaus, claiming that his brother, Andius, was captured by a Minotaur when the two of them were exploring a maze beneath the village Alturia.

Under the belief that many people have fallen victim to this creature, the duo are stunned to learn that no one knows what they're talking about, and as a result they're attacked by several men who think they're liars trying to manipulate the townspeople. When these men eventually turn up dead, all fingers point to Hercules and Iolaus as the perpetrators, although in reality it was the Minotaur.

Ultimately, the creature captures Iolaus, and Hercules confronts it in an effort to retrieve his friend. What he learns is that the Minotaur was once a human being transformed by Zeus a century earlier, and it is seeking vengeance against the king of the gods and will be happy to extract it from his son. Hercules ends up killing the creature in self-defense, but not before learning that its real name is Gryphus and that he is Hercules' half-brother; a man who had once used his charisma to control people, destroying anyone who didn't go along with his wishes. As penance for his misdeeds, Zeus transformed him.

HERCULES: THE LEGENDARY JOURNEYS YEAR ONE (1994)

All Episodes 43 Minutes in Length

Production Credits

Executive Producers: Sam Raimi
Robert Tapert
Co-executive Producer: John Schulian
Supervising Producer: Robert Bielak
Producer: Eric Gruendemann
Co-producer: David Eick
Created by: Christian Williams
Coordinating Producer: Bernadette Joyce
Line Producer: Chloe Smith
Associate Producer: Liz Friedman
Story Editor: Chris Manheim
Unit Production Manager: Eric Gruendemann
First Assistant Director: Andrew Merrifield
Second Assistant Director: Clare Richardson
Director of Photography: John Marafie
Edited by: David Blewitt
Visual Effects: Kevin O'Neill
Production Designer: Robert Gillies
Costume Designer: Nigla Dickson
New Zealand Casting: Diana Rowan
Stunt Coordinator: Peter Bell
Visual Effects: Flat Earth Productions, Inc.
Music: Joseph LoDuca

Regulars

Kevin Sorbo as Hercules
Michael Hurst as Iolaus/Charon

Semiregulars

Robert Trebor as Salmoneus
Elizabeth Hawthorne as Alcmene

Television Series Episode Guide

A note about this episode guide: Most of the behind-the-scenes commentaries featured in the following section were provided by former Hercules *co-executive producers John Schulian and Robert Bielak, the two men who have had more to do with the direction of the show's first three seasons than anyone. Sadly, both men have departed the show, Schulian because of a dispute with series star Kevin Sorbo and Bielak largely because he felt he had written himself out of the show, offering all that he could without falling into story repetition.*

Episode #1: "The Wrong Path"

Written by John Schulian
Directed by Doug Lefler
Guest Starring Clare Carey (Aegina), Elizabeth Hawthorne (Alcmene), and Mick Rose (Lycus)

When Hera destroys Hercules' wife and children in a horrific fireball—and Zeus does nothing to avert the tragedy—Hercules takes on the personal quest of destroying all of Hera's temples, simultaneously abandoning his mission to help those in need.

Unable to live with his best friend's decision, Iolaus attempts to carry the torch by helping villagers deal with a demon that is transforming the populace into stone. Unfortunately, he falls victim to the creature's powers and is transformed as well. Hearing of this, Hercules sets off to help him, turning the demon's abilities against itself, resulting in its own transformation and, as a result, the restoration of all its victims back to life.

At episode's end, Hercules becomes aware of the fact that his quest to destroy Hera need not come at the expense of those who come to him for help.

Behind the Scenes "The first one-hour episode," notes co-executive producer John Schulian, "in which I had the temerity to wipe out Hercules' wife and three kids with a fireball, I did that not because I'm sadistic or psychotic, but because a hero cannot go traipsing around ancient Greece saving everybody if he's got a wife and kids at home. It's very simple, and you should have heard the cries of dismay from the Black Tower at Universal. They were *horrified.* But if you look at classic kids' stories, it's *always* about somebody or some animal losing a parent and making his way in the world alone. That's what was different about this, and, honestly, it was the only way to do it. I believed that with all my heart. We argued about it, fought about it, and to his everlasting credit Bob Tapert was on my side from day one, and we finally won that battle. There are probably still people over there who were against this, but that's the way it had to be. Then Hercules goes off to get vengeance against Hera, his stepmother, and then his boy Iolaus goes off to do something Hercules should be doing and ends up being turned into stone by the She-Demon. Hercules hears about it and goes after him. At the end of the episode, Hercules brings his buddy back to life, and he realizes he's got to go out and see who else needs help. I really felt that was the show. It was a necessary episode—we had to find out where the show would go.

"That being said," he adds, "it was far from the most successful *Hercules* ever produced. I was still finding out who the character was. This was unlike writing a pilot in that when you write a pilot it's something that comes from inside you. In this case I was inheriting somebody else's character, and I was changing the show from what the two-hour movies had been. I just had a different approach to it. Ultimately the TV series was lighter than the movies, a little more comedic. The writing would be different, and that's because the writers were different. One of the other things with the pilot is that it was directed by a guy named Doug Lefler. Doug is a truly gifted storyboard artist in Hollywood. Rob hired him to direct the first episode, and I said, 'Are you crazy? You don't do that.' He said, 'Doug directed one of the two-hour movies,' and I said, 'That has nothing to do with directing a one-hour episode of television.' Because you move at a frantic pace when you're doing hour TV. You shoot seven pages of script a day, maybe eight. You're just flying, and you have to learn where to cut corners and where to spend your extra time. It's just a mess. But, no, no, Doug was going to do this. Well, the show—and I'm sure that Doug would tell you this himself—was not very well directed. Doug, to his credit, was smart enough when he saw what happened in the editing room with the show, and all the holes he had left, that the next episode he directed he did a terrific job on. Then he did one in the second season, 'The King of Thieves,' which he also came up with the story for—and it was a terrifically tight story—and he really understood the show and has turned out to be a really nice director. But the first episode was rotten."

Not surprisingly, Lefler doesn't agree. "We had new crew members for the series, a new director of photography, and we had to work a lot faster.

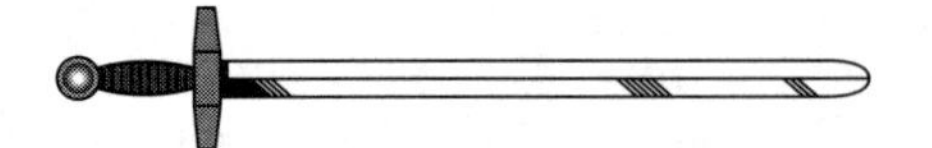

"We were taking bits of old techniques and bits of new techniques and combining them together, almost creating new forms of special effects."
—Director Doug Lefler

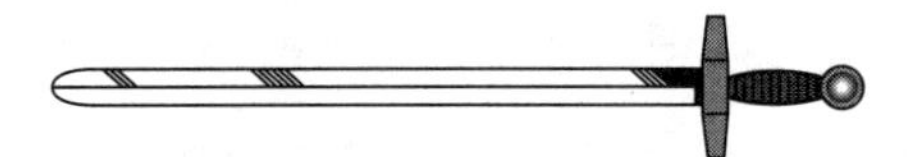

and what I could give to second unit, and I trusted the people doing second unit to put on film what I asked them to. Basically the lines of communication were good.

"There were a number of things about the first episode that were frustrating, that we

Other than that, the making of the film was very much the same. If you do your homework and you prepare carefully, you can estimate how many shots you'll get in a day. One of the things about both *Hercules* and *Xena* that is a wonderful advantage is that they have such an extensive second unit. Having been a second-unit director myself, I knew what I could hand off to them. Also, having been a second-unit director and a storyboard artist allowed me to plan out the sequences carefully, and I could do things that were a lot bigger than I otherwise might be able to do because I knew what I had to get first unit

didn't have time to get, that we had to simplify," continues Lefler. "I would have liked to have had more coverage of the scenes, more time to do more takes. It was a new enough situation that we didn't have all the mechanics down, so it went slower than we expected. That meant we got less coverage than we expected. A lot of times I had to simplify my plans, find ways to shoot things in a simpler way. It meant that I had to block-shoot scenes, which is if you have several scenes that are happening in the same place but you're intercutting it with something else, you shoot it all as if it was one scene.

"I liked the story line of the episode, and the darkness of it was kind of fun. After the movies it was nice to start it off that way to get people's attention. In retrospect I think I enjoyed the first half of the story more than the second half. Maybe it's my darker nature, but when Hercules was brooding and tortured, he interested me more. There was more meat to what we could do to the first half of the story as a result, and that has always been more interesting to me than straight-out action."

Episode #2: "Eye of the Beholder"

Written by John Schulian
Directed by John Kretchmer
Guest Starring Michael Mizrahi (Castor), Derek Ward (Ferret), David Press (Glaucus), and Ray Woolf (Chief Executioner)

While trying to elude the fifty daughters of King Thespius who want to bear his children, Hercules encounters a cyclops that is threatening a village by following Hera's bidding and altering the flow of a river to allow her vineyard to flourish. The creature has spent most of its life abused by the townspeople, so it doesn't have any problem assisting Hera until Hercules manages to negotiate a peace. Never a happy camper, Hera launches an attack with a group of warriors, not realizing that Hercules and the cyclops are working together to defeat them.

Behind the Scenes Reflects John Schulian, "That was the second episode that aired but the fifth one that was shot. It was directed by John Kretchmer, who was an assistant director on *Jurassic Park*—a really, truly, nice guy with a great sense of humor, and he understood forced perspective, where you shoot things at an angle. As far as the episode itself, I think it was the first one that captured the tone of what *Hercules* has become because it's kind of goofy, yet it has heart. It's about a misunderstood cyclops, a guy who's wreaking havoc in the countryside, but they all hate him because of what he is. Nobody's ever bothered to find out who he really is. They just see this big guy with one eye, and they hate him. The truth is, he's really a pretty good Joe. That's what that was about. It also has my favorite opening sequence in which Hercules is running and running, then stops to catch his breath.

He's being chased, and you simply can't believe that Hercules is running away from someone, but suddenly you hear a woman yell, 'There he is,' and you look to the top of the hill and you see all these beautiful women who are chasing Hercules because their father has decreed that each of them have to have a child by our boy Herc. And they are the running gag throughout the show.

"In this episode," he adds, "we also introduced Salmoneus, who became our resident schemer, played by an actor named Robert Trebor, who had played Son of Sam in the TV movie and was in *52 Pickup* as one of the truly creepy bad guys chasing Roy Scheider. A complete pain in the ass, and you can quote me. He drove me nuts, but I'll tell you something: He was great as Salmoneus. He was funny until he thought he had to rewrite his own lines. He was a great character to write because every time he appeared he had a new scam. In this episode he was a traveling toga salesman. Well, one of the jokes was that we never dressed anybody in togas on the show. He's trying to interest Hercules in wearing them, and he's saying, 'Look, you can put out your own line.' Well, *that* is what we always had him doing, coming up with a new scam. He sold real estate, he had a self-actualization program, he was the world's first celebrity biographer—we had him do everything, and it was really fun to try and come up with something for him.

"Having told you all this, I get a phone call from an executive at Universal who shall go unnamed who said, 'You can't shoot this episode.' 'Excuse me?' 'This is just too light and frothy.' Of course I went off in my inimitable fashion in a conversation punctuated by many expletives. Ultimately I said, 'Look, I want to do this, more importantly Rob Tapert wants to do this. If you don't like it, you call him in New Zealand and tell him we're not doing it. He's the executive producer.' I never heard from him again until, six months later, this executive was gracious enough to call me and say that he had made a terrible mistake, that the episode was terrific, and at that point I think it was our highest-rated Hercules ever. It was an episode that really worked."

Episode #3: "The Road to Calydon"

Written by Andrew Dettman and Daniel Truly
Directed by Doug Lefler
Guest Starring Norman Forsey (The Seer), John Sumner (Broteas), Portia Dawson (Jana), Christopher Sunoa (Ixion), Peter Dowley (Epitalon), Sela Brown (Leda), Stephen Papps (Teles), Andrew Lawrence (Odeus), Maggie Turner (Hecate), and Bruce Allpress (Old Man)

A blind seer leads Hercules to a village being ravaged by a series of unexplained, violent storms that, the seer announces, are the result of someone stealing Hera's chalice. Hercules, perhaps getting some pleasure in ticking off his stepmother, agrees to help the people to Calydon.

Things don't get easy, however, when they embark on their journey. The storms follow them, accompanied by raining rocks, Hera's warriors, and a battle to the death between Hercules and a winged creature known as a Stymphalian Bird. Surviving this struggle, Hercules comes to the conclusion that the Chalice must be amongst the crowd. One man, Broteas, admits that he has stolen the chalice to remove Hera's control over the village. Taking the dark power upon himself, Hercules holds the chalice as he leads the people into Calydon, a city whose strange properties nullify Hera's curse.

Behind the Scenes "One of our less successful episodes," says John Schulian simply. "I think when you look at the episode you don't really end up liking anybody. The quicksand is a hoot because it's like gravel or oatmeal or something. I didn't think the script ever really worked. I thought the Stymphalian Bird could have been done better. We have the blind seer in this one, and I had to take a lot of cheap jokes about blind guys out of the script. I don't have the fondest memories of this episode."

Adds director Doug Lefler, "It was probably the least satisfying of all the *Hercules* and *Xena* episodes I've done, only because the story line didn't get you very emotionally involved with the characters. I found years later when I watched it I didn't care that much about the adventure as a result. And we were still feeling our way, getting used to what we could accomplish. What I remember mostly about that episode was that it was a road show; they were traveling from one place to another. It was the middle of the rainy season, and everywhere we went when we started shooting, the ground might look firm and safe, but after a crew had walked across it for about an hour, everything turned to mud. I remember when they were going through the swamp, which I felt didn't look like a dangerous swamp on film but actually was in reality, as it was such a quagmire. Also, for reasons of economy it was a lot easier to make sandals for all those extras than it was to make boots, but imagine those poor actors walking through mud with open-toed sandals. It was not fun for them, but they were all real troopers."

Episode # 4: "The Festival of Dionysis"

Written by Andrew Dettman and Daniel Truly
Directed by Peter Ellis
Guest Starring Noel Trevarthan (King Iphicles), Ilona Rodgers (Queen Camilla), Norman Forsey (The Seer), Mark Newham (Ares), Martyn Sanderson (Priest), Johnny Blick (Nestor), Warren Carl (Pentheus), Kartina Hobbs (Marysa), and Todd Rippon (Gudrun)

Hercules is approached by Prince Nestor, who claims that someone is trying to assassinate his father, King Iphicles. Trying to do the right thing, Herc checks out the situation but finds himself a pawn in a tragedy of Shakespearean proportions when it's discovered that Nestor's brother, Prince Pentheus (working in collaboration with Ares, the god of war), is actually planning on killing their father so he can assume the throne.

To this end, Pentheus has Hercules and Nestor imprisoned, though they manage to escape, en route battling a giant eel and ultimately aided by the seer Hercules met in the previous episode. In the end, Pentheus is exposed, and Nestor becomes the chosen future king.

Episode #5: "Ares"

Written by Steve Roberts
Directed by Harley Cokeliss
Guest Starring Cory Everson (Atalanta), Peter Malloch (Titus), Marsie Wipani (Janista),

Callum Stembridge (Aurelius), Taungaroa Emile (Ximenos), and Mark Newham (Ares)

Arriving in the village of Fallia to inform Janista and her son, Titus, that her husband has died in battle, Hercules tries to help the teenager cope with the loss of his father. Unfortunately, the boy falls under the sway of the mysterious Aurelius, who is turning misguided teenage boys into a new, young army for Ares. Adding insult to injury, he tries tricking Titus into believing that Hercules is actually the one responsible for his father's death.

Hercules must rescue Titus before it's too late and stop the plans of both Aurelius and Ares.

Behind the Scenes Says John Schulian, "The single, most embarrassing moment of my writing life. It was, quite simply, a script that never should have been shot. We were in a mode—not me, because I believe that you throw out scripts, even though it winds up costing you money. This was a script that in its story stages was incomprehensible, and it didn't get any better. We should have scrapped it, but Rob Tapert didn't want to throw any scripts out, so we wound up shooting it. I can't tell you how many revisions and rewrites this went through. Ultimately I wound up taking a pass at it before it was shot. To be very blunt, that was like putting a coat of paint on a turd. It's just an awful, awful episode. When we have the Ares monster and he has a stocking cap on his head—*everybody* dropped the ball on this one, from Rob to me to the writer, Steve Roberts, to the special effects monster guys. It's a horrible hour of television, and all prints of it should be burned.

"However, kids love that episode because it is about kids. They like it, and we introduced in that episode Atalanta, the lady blacksmith played by Cory Everson, who is a female bodybuilder of international renown. In my ignorance I did not know who she was before I started working on *Hercules.* She's a walking special effect. She has an arm-wrestling scene with Hercules which is quite memorable. She distracts Hercules with her cleavage, and it's hysterical. How we ever got the episode on the air with the costume she was wearing is astounding. It's quite revealing, particularly from the rear, and there's a moment when she's walking away from the camera in one scene and says, 'No buts about it.' I'm not a prude, okay? But *I* was offended by it. Anyway, in that episode Cory's really not very good. She's astounding in a physical sense, but her acting leaves much to be desired. Then, when you see her in an episode called 'Let the Games Begin,' she's quite good. She really improved. She's not Katherine Hepburn in her prime or anything, but she was just much better, a nice little comedic flair, much more comfortable on camera."

Episode #6: "As Darkness Falls"

Written by Robert Bielak
Directed by George Mendeluk
Guest Starring Lucy Lawless (Lyla), Robert Trebor (Salmoneus), Cliff Curtis (Nemis), Peter Muller (Deric), Jaqueline Collen (Penelope), and Mark Ferguson (Craesus)

Weddings and Hercules don't mix, as this episode emphasizes when the demigod attends the nuptials of Penelope and Marcus. No sooner has he arrived in Nespa than he is approached by the beautiful Lyla, who wants him to stay there with her. When he refuses, she fills his wine with a drug that begins to affect his eyesight.

Complicating matters is the arrival of a trio of centaurs who abduct both Penelope and one of the bridesmaids. Despite his failing eyesight, Hercules, along with Salmoneus, who has become a real estate agent of sorts, sets off in pursuit. In the end, there's a lot of self-sacrifice and the realization for Lyla that she actually loves one of the centaurs and in reality has no interest in Hercules.

Behind the Scenes "Bob Bielak's first script," enthuses John Schulian. "It's really about bigotry involving the centaurs. Bob wrote a terrific script. I remember he dropped it off on a Friday evening, and I sat and read it immediately and called David Eick, and he said, 'How is it?' I said, 'I've read eight pages so far, and it's in English!' It was a good script, a really solid effort. In all honesty it earned Bob my undying gratitude because I just really needed a good script at that point, and he came through.

"It's also a really good episode. Salmoneus is in it, but it's not a comedic episode really. It's about serious stuff, and you'll see Lucy Lawless as the girl who tries to seduce Hercules. Lucy was good. She just looked great and did a good job. Anyway, the episode is notable for Lucy and Bob saving my life."

"I had the temerity to wipe out Hercules' wife and three kids with a fireball. . . . You should have heard the cries of dismay from the Black Tower at Universal."
—Co-executive Producer John Schulian

Robert Bielak explains that this episode was the result of a verbal pitch while he was still a freelancer trying to sell to the show. "I'm not real good on my feet; I'm not the greatest pitcher in the world and have often thought that I should hire an actor to go in and pitch the stories for me and I'll execute the scripts," he admits. "I went in and pitched a group of ideas, none of them really hit, though there was a glimmer in one. Rob Tapert said they wanted to do a story about centaurs, so I married one of my ideas with centaurs. They never asked me to pitch again. What they did was ask me to fax in my ideas from that point on. After that I would gather up three ideas, fax them in, and we'd take it from there.

"The first three I wrote I thought worked really well," he says. "This one was called the testosterone episode because it was deemed the most Herculean at the time. He'd been blinded in the middle of this thing and was still going to go after this guy and do the right thing. Robert Trebor was in that too, and, again, he tends to improvise and angers the writers. The good news is that many of his improvisations are good. I think I got him early on, and he tended to stick closer to the scripts early on than he did later. He was just a funny character. You got to do all your agent and lawyer jokes with him—the crass, money-hungry guy. Again, the shows were fun to write because you weren't limited to one thing.

"The interesting thing about *Hercules* is that when I came in to it there was no real reference point in terms of how to do the show," says Bielak. "There was really nothing out there that preceded *Hercules* that said, 'This is how they did it, this is how we're going to do it.' You were kind of on your own, and I sort of let it all hang out. I don't know what kind of sense of humor I have, whether it's wacky or bizarre, but I never felt that I had to filter it or put a reign on it. Put it out there in a first draft and see what they think about it. Invariably if it made the producers laugh, it stayed. So you could push things as much as you wanted, and that was a nice feeling that you wouldn't get slapped down if you tried something different."

Episode #7: "Pride Comes Before a Brawl"

Written by Steve Roberts
Directed by Peter Ellis
Guest Starring Lisa Chappell (Lydia), Karen Witter (Nemesis), John Dybvig (Rankor), Jeff Gane (Rak), and David Stott (Boatman)

A rivalry forms between Hercules and Iolaus, with the latter determined to prove that he doesn't need the former's constant protection and rescue efforts. Iolaus is given no choice but to back up his claims when Nemesis, the goddess of retribution, sets her sights on him because he has exhibited the sin of pride. As a result, he is captured by phony satyrs but manages to escape with a fellow prisoner named Lydia and take on a humongous eel and multi-headed hydra. By episode's end, he has indeed proven himself quite capable.

Behind the Scenes Offers John Schulian, "Steve Roberts, bless his heart, on this one must have taken ten passes before the story was ready. I was working on a pilot at the same time. I remember I would do my *Hercules* work from eight-thirty or nine until four in the afternoon and would eat my lunch at my desk every day, and in the evenings I would work on my pilot. And every day Steve would bring me the story, I'd give him all kinds of notes, and he'd go back and he'd bring it back, then I'd give him more notes and he'd bring it back again. I thought he was going to kill himself or kill me, but he just hung in there, and finally we got the story in shape to show other people. It turned out to be a good episode. Lisa Chappel is quite good in it. She's very charming, and she's very good with Michael Hurst because they're off together while Hercules is reunited with an old flame of his, the hit woman of the gods—Nemesis—played by Karen Witter. The problem is we couldn't find the right Nemesis. Karen Witter, who was just wonderful in the casting session, got over there and had none of the life, the charm, or whatever that had made us cast her. I had no idea what happened. Lisa Chappel was swell, and we wound up using her in a number of other episodes as other characters, and she was always good. As far as that is concerned, I guess we were kind of like a little traveling theater company with the same actors playing different characters. Hercules, Iolaus, and Salmoneus are the only constants in the show."

Episode #8: "The March to Freedom"

Written by Adam Armus and Nora Kay Foster
Directed by Harley Cokeliss
Guest Starring Lucy Liu (Oi-Lan), Nathaniel Lees (Cyrus), Stig Eldred (Belus), Elizabeth Hawthorne (Alcmene), Maya Dallziel (Mother), and Joanna Barrett (Pretty Girl)

Hercules' efforts to buy and then free a woman, Oi-Lan, from slave traders backfires in the sense that her lover, Cyrus, has also been sold as a slave and she wants to rescue him. Herc agrees to help, unaware of the fact that Cyrus has escaped and is determined to kill the man who purchased his woman. Through a series of misadventures, Hercules is shoved over a cliff, and the couple are recaptured by the slave traders. Hercules, who has (naturally) survived his little trip, frees Cyrus, and together they take on the traders.

The episode concludes with Hercules giving Cyrus and Oi-Lan the land that had belonged to his family before they were massacred by Hera's actions. It is a place that can never bring him joy, but it just might give these lovers a new chance in life.

Behind the Scenes "The writers were friends of Rob Tapert who had to deliver their first television script at the speed of light," says John Schulian. "Nobody ever had to work in less fair circumstances, and they ended up doing an alright job. Harley Cokeliss, the director, gave us a really cinematic opening sequence, and we used some stuff from the Chinese action movies with guys flying through the air, which was the Rob Tapert touch. He loves those movies. That's an episode that I thought actually worked pretty well. It was a difficult one, but it worked."

Episode #9: "The Warrior Princess"

Written by John Schulian
Directed by Bruce Seth Green
Guest Starring Lucy Lawless (Xena), Elizabeth Hawthorne (Alcmene), Bill Johnson (Petrakis), and Michael Dwyer (Theodorus)

The warrior princess Xena comes to the conclusion that the only thing standing between her and ultimate power is Hercules, so she hatches a plan that will, hopefully, turn Hercules and Iolaus against each other and, hopefully in her mind, result in the death of the demigod. What she doesn't expect, however, is that Hercules' feelings of loyalty are so strong that he will not hurt a friend. Xena is defeated, vowing to return some day and finish the job she started.

Behind the Scenes "Welcome to Xenaland," proclaims John Schulian, who is credited with co-creating the character with Robert Tapert. "Rob and David Eick came to me after I had done 'Wrong Path' and 'Eye of the Beholder' and said, 'Okay, now you've done something light and frothy, and we'd like something darker.' I wanted to do an episode about the woman who came between Hercules and Iolaus, and Rob always wanted to do one about a great female warrior, thus Xena was born. Xena wants to kill Hercules and be the world's greatest warrior, so she seduces Iolaus and leads him away. Hercules figures out what she's up to and goes to fetch him back, and all sorts of things happen before they're reunited and chase Xena away.

"I don't know where the name *Xena* came from," he adds, "but I knew I wanted her name to start with an *X*. Later I was at my dry cleaners—and by this time Xena was a cultural phenomenon—and one of the guys behind the counter said, 'Xena is a very popular name for women in Russia.' I had no idea, I just thought it was a cool brainstorm. It just worked. I think it was Rob's favorite episode that first season and might still be his favorite. It's just one of those things that worked.

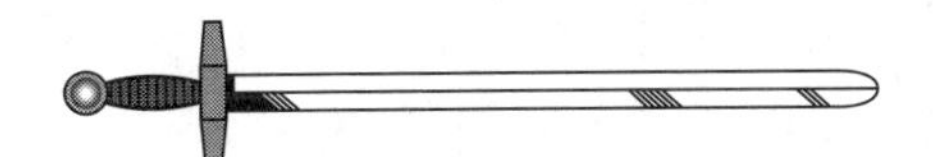

"The amazing thing to me about Hercules is the way that the various episodes are up, down, and all over the place. Some of the episodes should never have hit the airwaves. Despite the constantly changing quality of the various episodes, the show definitely filled a void. People were really looking for something like this show."

—Co-executive Producer John Schulian

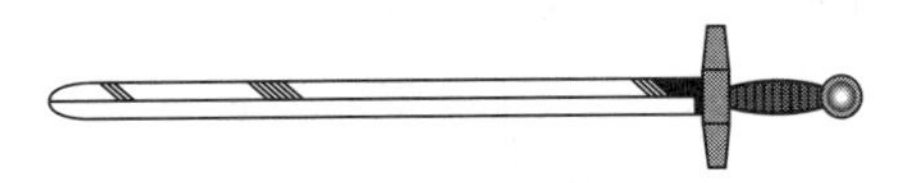

"Actually there's a story behind Lucy Lawless' being cast in the role. We originally cast an actress named Vanessa Angel. Vanessa at that time was the star of a USA Network series called *Weird Science,* and she went on to star in a movie with Woody Harrelson and Randy Quaid called *Kingpin.* A beautiful girl, truly gorgeous. Small and delicate and fragile, and none of those things we've come to associate with Xena. Rob trotted her off to martial arts lessons and horseback riding lessons. This would be the first show we would shoot in 1995. We were going to shoot the three *Xena* episodes together even though they didn't air sequentially because we had the actress. She said, 'I'm going home to London to spend the holidays to be with my family, and I'll come back to Los Angeles on my way to New Zealand.' Fine, you can't get in the way of holiday bliss with the family. Now the week between Christmas and New Year's is, traditionally, the deadest week in Hollywood. There's *nobody* in town, nobody but old John writing the next episode of *Hercules.* Rob and David were all doing their editing chores and fighting whatever demons they were fighting that particular episode. Well, we get a call from Vanessa, coughing and saying that her doctor says she can't travel. Well, thank you very much, my dear.

"So, we're stuck. We don't have an actress, and I don't know what we're going to do. Who else read for the part? What B-movie actresses have you seen? Who came in and read for *Darkman*? At one point we took a run at Kim Delaney, who has gone on to win an Emmy [for *NYPD Blue*]. I said, 'What about Lucy Lawless?' and David Eick had always been a big Lucy Lawless fan. I think Rob was up for it—I know he was—and he tracked her down and she was on vacation. I think she was mining for gold in Australia, and she said, 'Oh, that would be cool,' in this great New Zealand accent. You know what? She came back, she played the part. I saw the first day's dailies, and she's riding a horse, swinging a sword, and kicking the crap out of people—well, there's Xena. Had no idea that it would go on to become the phenomenon that it has become."

Episode #10: "The Gladiator"

Written by Robert Bielak

Directed by Garth Maxwell

Guest Starring Tony Todd (Gladius), Ian Mune (Menos Maxius), Alison Bruce (Postera), Kyrin Hall (Felicita), Mark Nua (Skoros), Stuart Turner (Leulia), Nigel Harbrow (Turkos), Gabriel Pendergast (Spagos), Tawny Kitaen (Deianeira), Jeffrey Thomas (Dellicus), Ray Bishop

(Rankus), and Jonathan Bell-Booth (Traveller)

By saving a woman (Felicita) and her child from would-be kidnappers, Hercules and Iolaus ultimately allow themselves to get arrested to find her husband, the gladiator known as Gladius. They learn that he is being held by the cruel Menas Maxius, who has grown tired of men battling animals and has decided to up the ante by having men battle one another to the death for his own amusement.

Hercules feels he's got the upper hand, until Maxius takes both Felicita and Iolaus prisoner and threatens to kill them unless Herc and Gladius battle each other until one is victorious.

Behind the Scenes "I think this was an episode where I really knew what I wanted it to be," John Schulian explains. "It's about an athlete aging, and as an old sportswriter, I had seen a lot of that; guys hanging on, their bodies creaking. And this is a guy separated from his family, and Hercules ends up defending the guy. Bob did a terrific job with it, tapping into what I was looking for, and he understood the show. Tony Todd was really good in the part, and the director did a great job."

Offers the episode's writer, Robert Bielak, "I suppose that was our take on *Spartacus,* though, funny enough, I'd never seen *Spartacus* before I decided to do the story. I guess it's because I had kind of lumped it into all those old big biblical epics. I'd seen *Ben Hur,* and that was good enough for me, and I didn't need to see anything else. I'd seen parts of others, and they didn't measure up, so I wasn't interested in those kinds of movies. Somehow along the way I've never seen *Spartacus,* but it worked its way in there. The other thing is that with the humor and some of the situations, we were playing it that way. For instance, Salmoneus was the first agent: 'Hey, listen, when you hang up these animals, can I open up a shop and represent you?' That's how we played 'The Gladiator'—up until this time it had been played man against animal, and now the turn was coming where that wasn't enough. So it became men against men and therefore became the perfect thing for Hercules to become involved in. You know,

'We're talking about humanity here, and I won't let this happen.' There was some good stuff about the aging gladiator and the guy who should hang up his spikes, but there's something about that arena, the show, and when the crowd cheers all of a sudden the adrenaline comes back and he grows like six inches because people are spurring him on. Some good stuff in the episode. Good heart things and a little bit of social commentary. The humor tended to get lost a little bit in that; it wasn't a humorous episode. The most we had was a cook named Spagos."

Episode #11: "The Vanishing Dead"

Written by Andrew Dettman and Daniel Truly
Directed by Bruce Campbell
Guest Starring Erik Thomson (King Daulin), Reb Brown (Jarton), Amber-Jane Raab (Poene), Richard Vette (Aelon), and Chris McDowell (Krytus)

Ares, who isn't happy unless he's sitting back and watching battle, manipulates King Daulin and his sister, Peona, into a savage war between their respective armies, a war whose results are enigmatic in that the dead are mysteriously vanishing. Shortly before the final battle—which will undoubtedly result in tremendous casualties on both sides—Hercules and Iolaus find Ares in a secret cave and go up against him and his dog of war, who has been devouring the corpses of the dead. After the battle, Herc must convince Daulin and Peona of the truth behind the string-puller in their war.

Behind the Scenes "Bruce was the star of the *Evil Dead* films and was a friend of Rob and Sam's," notes John Schulian. "We used an actor named Reb Brown in this, who we had used in an episode of *Miami Vice.* Reb just wasn't very good in this. He's a handsome guy, and he's really put together, but he doesn't have a voice that goes with the rest of him. It's like what they say about pretty girls who can't act: God doesn't give with both hands. The story was a nice enough idea, but it didn't all come together."

Episode #12: "The Gauntlet"

Written by Robert Bielak
Directed by Jack Perez
Guest Starring Lucy Lawless (Xena), Robert Trebor (Salmoneus), Matthew Chamberlain

(Darphus), Dean O'Gorman (Iloran), and Peter Daube (Spiros)

When her first officer, Darphus, turns against her because she refuses to kill women and children in their raids, Xena finds herself an outcast from her own army. She turns to Hercules for help, and although he is initially unwilling to team up with a former enemy, he ultimately relents. In the end, Xena goes one-on-one with Darphus, killing the man. But Ares, who essentially liked the man's style, resurrects him so that the man can see retribution against both Hercules and Xena.

"The single, most embarrassing moment of my writing life. It was, quite simply, a script that never should have been shot."

—Co-executive Producer John Schulian on "Ares"

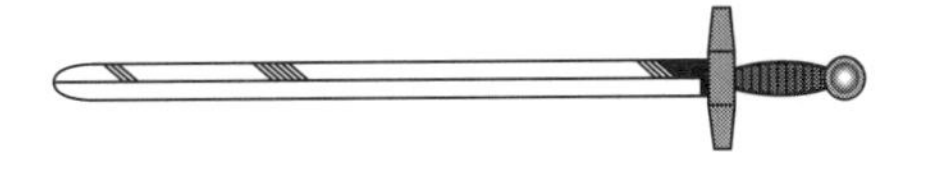

Behind the Scenes John Schulian points out that director Jack Perez was reportedly uptight throughout much of the episode's shooting, often pausing to throw up in the bushes. "I actually thought, having said that about old Jack, the episode looked great," he says. "Whether that's Jack's work or the DP or our line producer leaning on the right people, it looked great. The problem was that it wasn't an episode of *Hercules.* It was so dark and so hyperviolent that it just didn't fit in to what we were doing. When you think of *Xena* now, it's a much darker show than *Hercules.* An episode with this tone and theme would probably work better on *Xena* than it did on *Hercules.* The show really did look great: Xena is cast out of her army, she's made to run the gauntlet, and I can't tell you how hard we had to edit the gauntlet down to make it palatable because we had a gang of guys beating

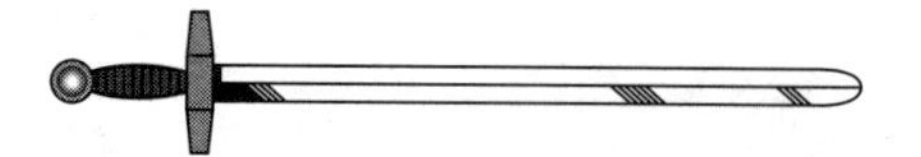

"One thing ['Prince Hercules'] did was to get Kevin out of his leather pants. Kevin got to wear a princely outfit, which he was eternally grateful for."
—Co-executive Producer Robert Bielak

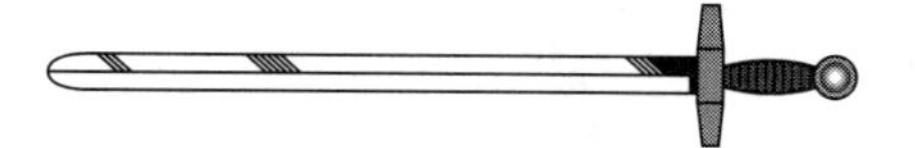

the weeping dog meat out of a woman. Even if it's Xena, the toughest woman in the world, there's still something that really strikes you wrong about it. So that was very, very dicey. There's a funny moment with Salmoneus in drag trying to hide from these guys and pretending that he's the bearded lady. That was a nice light moment there. That's one of those episodes I like, but I want to put an asterisk by that statement because it's so different from *Hercules.*

"I think the character of Xena herself just makes things darker. She comes from a different place than Hercules. It was also a green director, not really knowing that you're not out to make a movie; you're not making something that stands by itself. You're making something that fits into a larger body of work. I'm sure Jack was so busy trying to figure out where the camera should be or whether he had anything to tell the actors, he wasn't thinking about the realities of the series. If Bruce Seth Green, for example, had directed that episode, it would have been different. It probably would have still been dark, but not *as* dark."

According to Robert Bielak, the story for "The Gauntlet" came largely from Robert Tapert. "He had this female warrior princess thing he wanted to do," he explains. "At the time nobody really thought of it as a series or anything. By that point I had gotten two under my belt, so they felt comfortable with me. First we were going to do a two-parter, and then they decided to stretch it out to a three-parter, and it was decided that John would do the first and last and I would do the middle part. They wanted to get Hercules and Iolaus at odds with each other, introduce this female warrior that, again, you hadn't seen much of before on TV. John introduced her, I took her a little bit further, and John finished it off. Lo and behold, there was Lucy and there was Xena.

"That episode did turn out pretty dark," Bielak adds, concurring with Schulian. "I think it was actually darker than the script was. The director we had, it was one of his early TV ventures, but he had this great vision of what the show should look like. It was a departure of what the show had looked like before; it was just very dark and very bloody. The beginning of the episode where they attacked the village was like feature-quality material. They only used like forty extras, but it looked like four hundred. He just had some great stuff in there; the pillage of the village was amazing, and, as I said, it was darker than it was scripted. He went that extra step where I think if I had directed it or someone else had, we would have pulled back a little bit. He had singed bodies and stuff still standing upright, and where poor Xena runs the gauntlet and gets beaten is just awful stuff to watch. It was actually toned down from what was in the dailies. We were looking at the dailies saying, 'Jeez, there are kids watching this show.' It wasn't as if he went off and did his own thing. It was all there in the script, he just shaded it more. Again, an episode that worked, and I liked what it had to say about loyalty, and it showed that Xena was a killer but she still had her code."

Episode #13: "Unchained Heart"

Written by John Schulian

Directed by Bruce Seth Green

Guest Starring Lucy Lawless (Xena), Robert Trebor (Salmoneus), Matthew Chamberlain (Darphus), Stephen Papps (Pylendor), Mervyn Smith (Village Elder), Robert Pollock (Villager), Shane Dawson (First Warrior), Ian Harrop (Camp Boss), Margo Gada (Quintas), Bruce Allpress (Eros), David Mercer (Warrior), Gordon Hatfield (Lieutenant), and Campbell Rousselle (Sentry)

The resurrected Darphus and his army begin seeking revenge against Hercules and Xena, starting with the kidnapping of the jack-of-many-trades Salmoneus. Naturally, Herc, Xena, and Iolaus manage to rescue him and put a final stop to Darphus, all of which has the effect of rehabilitating Xena, who decides to help others and sets off, alone, to face her new destiny.

Behind the Scenes "Xena gets religion, so to speak," says John Schulian of this episode. "I had no idea at this point that Xena would be spun off into her own series. We had planned an arc in which she goes from bad in 'The Warrior Princess' to becoming an outcast in 'The Gauntlet' to winding up on the side of what's good and right in 'Unchained Heart.' This was a full episode because we had Iolaus and Salmoneus together, which was an unhappy marriage between Michael Hurst and Robert Trebor because Robert Trebor, if you watch these episodes closely, is a shameless scene stealer, always mugging for the camera. They should have used tranquilizer darts on him. He's a handful, that's all I can tell you. He and Michael did not have the best time working together. But they're still fun, both the characters and the actors. And this episode was lighter than 'The Gauntlet.' Of course, *anything* would be lighter than 'The Gauntlet.' But it still had action and was about the conversion of this woman, getting her straightened out. It is definitely an episode of *Hercules*.

"You know, in talking about these episodes, I don't think I've mentioned Kevin Sorbo at all. He's really the rock on which all of these are built. He's a guy who can do the humor. There's one episode where he visits his family's graves, and he's very good; he's surprisingly moving. You just don't think of that coming from a big hunky action star. Kevin could surprise you now and again, by tapping into that kind of emotion. He really was the right guy to play Hercules. Without him the show would spin off its axis. By talking about all of these other things, I don't intend to demean him. He is consistently good in the show."

HERCULES: THE LEGENDARY JOURNEYS YEAR TWO (1995)

All Episodes 43 Minutes in Length

Production Credits

Executive Producers: Sam Raimi
Robert Tapert
Co-executive Producer: John Schulian
Supervising Producer: Robert Bielak
Producer: Eric Gruendemann
Co-producer: David Eick
Coordinating Producer: Bernadette Joyce
Line Producer: Chloe Smith
Associate Producer: Liz Friedman
Story Editor: Chris Manheim
Created by: Christian Williams
Unit Production Manager: Eric Gruendemann
First Assistant Director: Andrew Merrifield
Second Assistant Directors: Clare Richardson
Charlie Haskell
Director of Photography: John Marafie
Edited by: David Blewitt
Visual Effects: Kevin O'Neill
Production Designer: Robert Gillies
Costume Designer: Nigla Dickson
New Zealand Casting: Diana Rowan
Stunt Coordinator: Peter Bell
Music: Joseph LoDuca
Visual Effects: Flat Earth Productions, Inc.

Regulars

Kevin Sorbo as Hercules
Michael Hurst as Iolaus/Charon

Semiregulars

Robert Trebor as Salmoneus
Liddy Holloway as Alcmene

Episode #14: "The King of Thieves"

Written and Directed by Doug Lefler
Guest Starring Bruce Campbell (Autolycus), Martyn Sanderson (King Menelaus), and Lisa Chappel (Dirce)

When Iolaus is accused of stealing King Menelaus' treasure, he is sentenced to die. It is up to Hercules to find the real thief, a brilliant escape artist named Autolycus, who has become known, in more recent years, as the King of Thieves. Herc tracks him down to a mysteriously empty castle that is guarded by a serpent and is filled with a wide variety of traps that the duo must traverse by working together. Autolycus must be taken back to King Menelaus so that Iolaus will be spared, but the man proves that standing trial for his crimes will be difficult—when he effortlessly escapes yet again.

Behind the Scenes "Doug Lefler wrote and directed this," says John Schulian. "He had come a long way, had learned from his mistakes. I think when he saw what the editors went through on the first show he shot and what he had left them without, then he really learned. He was very smart about it and just stumped if the scene had more than two people in it. We like the cameras to move a little bit, and he would just plant it in one place. That growth was nice to see. Anyway, in this he came up with the story, and of all the freelancers I worked with, this was the most polished story I got from any of them. I thought the episode turned out real well, and Bruce Campbell was really good. He got into playing Autolycus, the king of thieves, and he and Kevin worked really well together. Just a fun episode, and Bruce just sparked."

Writer/director Doug Lefler notes, "That was probably the most enjoyable of all the experiences I had. By writing the script it allowed me to have a lot of time to think about it, and I started doing my preproduction work at least a month in advance. By that point, we had gotten the system down, and I knew everybody there, I had a good handle on what cast was available. I'd actually cast the show and picked most of the locations before I even went down there. I had a good communication with the production designer at that point. I'd faxed him my storyboards in advance, and he faxed me back drawings of the sets. We did a lot of stuff before it got there. The costume designer went to great lengths to fax me drawings. Since it was the first show of the season, everybody got a jump on it; their entire attention was focused on it, which made it fun. John Schulian was a great help in getting the script whipped into shape from where it was when it was submitted. Also helping was that I had written a story in which most of the scenes were between two characters, and that made it more containable and controllable.

"The thing that interested me about this story line was creating a situation that had a moral dilemma for Hercules. If it was just a physical obstacle, we always knew he would overcome it because he's the strongest man on earth. By creating a situation where he has to save the life of his friend, but in order to do that it will mean the sacrifice of somebody else, it created a moral dilemma where the outcome wasn't obvious. That made the story more interesting for me, and I always felt that those stories worked better for Hercules when we had some sort of moral issue that had to be dealt with."

Episode #15: "All That Glitters"

Written by Craig Volk
Directed by Garth Maxwell
Guest Starring Robert Trebor (Salmoneus), Jennifer Leah-Ward (Voluptua), Tracy Lindsey (Flaxen), Noel Trevarthen (King Midas), Terry Batchelor (Segallus), Margaret-Mary Hollins (Hispides), Max Cryer (Barker), Alexander Gandar (Tacharius), Joseph Greer (Romanus), David Scott (Paraicles), Peter Rowley (Buffoon), Dale Corlett (Thaddeus), James O'Farrell (Eisenkopf), and Ray Sefo (Alee)

King Midas is manipulated into using his wealth and influence to open a gambling establishment in which the risks are, quite literally, life and death. In other words, the crowd is betting whether someone will survive a situation. When Hercules comes upon this place, he's horrified by what's going on there and intervenes, saving the life of a young boy who in all likelihood would have died. Both Midas and his partner, Voluptua, want the son of Zeus to be a starring act at the casino, but he refuses. He does participate in a boxing match because it's the only way Voluptua won't kill Midas, but he uses the arena as an opportunity to convince the townspeople that the casino is wrong and that they should tear it down—which they do.

Behind the Scenes "Our Las Vegas episode," muses John Schulian. "We had read about what had happened when gambling casinos get put in small towns or bizarre places throughout the country. The bottom line is, there's no pot of gold there. Even a city like New Orleans, where the riverboat casinos just bombed completely. I think the writer, Craig

Volk, is from South Dakota, and so he had seen what towns had gone through when they opened casinos or they opened on Indian reservations. That's what inspired this. Not the world's greatest episode."

Episode #16: "What's in a Name?"

Written by Michael Marks
Directed by Bruce Campbell
Guest Starring Kevin Smith (Iphicles), Kenneth McGregor (Gorgus), Simone Kessell (Rena), Ross Duncan (Pallaeus), Paul Glover (Josephus), Liddy Holloway (Alcmene), Lewis Martin (Priest), Jon Watson (Hawker), Simon Prast (First Soldier), Jason Garner (Young Soldier), Bernard Moodi (Old Man), and John McNee (Soldier)

Hercules goes up against his mortal half-brother, Iphicles, when he discovers that the man is pretending to be him in order to impress a woman. And, while pretending to be the demigod, Iphicles has supposedly been lending Hercules' good name to a warlord named Gorgus. In the end, when the brothers must work together to overcome other-worldly threats, Iphicles realizes that he must be true to himself—which is, it turns out, enough to win the heart of the young woman he loves.

Episode #17: "Siege at Naxos"

Written by Darrell Fetty
Directed by Stephen L. Posey
Guest Starring Brian Thompson (Goth), Ray Woolf (Bledar), Rebecca Hobbs (Elora), Patrick Smyth (Charidon), Robert Harte (Dax), Richard Adams (Argeas), and Zo Hartley (Patron)

Hercules and Iolaus manage to apprehend the warlord named Goth and plan on bringing him to trial in Athens when they learn that the man's brother, Bledar, has an army at his disposal to free him. The trio end up at a fortress that houses a father and daughter, Charidon and Elora, who help them fight off the army, managing to give the illusion that there are vast forces within the fortress. They must somehow escape without revealing the truth to Bledar and his soldiers.

Behind the Scenes Points out John Schulian, "The episode's writer, Darrell Fetty, came out to California as an actor and worked in a lot of John Milius movies, including *The Wind and the Lion* and *Big Wednesday,* and then slowly turned to writing. This was our version of *Rio Bravo,* and Darrell, of course, is a big western movie fan. I really liked the script. I don't think Rob Tapert liked it as much as I did; I think he had far more problems. One of the many problems outside writers have coming in is that they had no way to gauge the size or scope or potential cost of an episode. So they would write things, and our response would be, 'That would be great if our budget was three million dollars an episode, but it's not.' But I think this episode was real big, and we had to keep bringing it down to size. One of the show's virtues is that we really did put a lot on the screen. I thought the shows by and large always looked good. We were shooting these things in seven or seven and a half days, just flying. In the end, I thought the episode was reasonably successful."

There was really nothing that preceded Hercules that said, 'This is how they did it, this is how we're going to do it.' You were kind of on your own, and I sort of let it all hang out."

—Co-executive Producer Robert Bielak

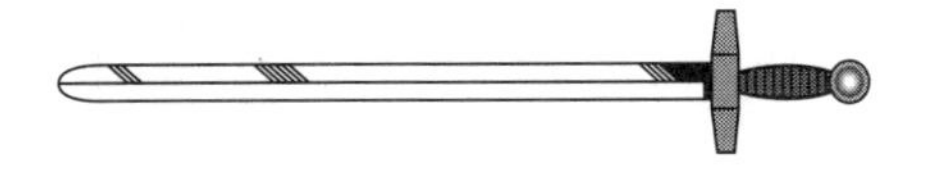

Episode #18: "Outcast"

Written by Robert Bielak

Directed by Bruce Seth Green

Guest Starring Lucy Lawless (Lyla), Peter Muller (Deric), Neil Holt (Merkus), Jon Brazier (Jakar), Rose Dube (Leuriphone), James Croft (Kefor), Chris Bailey (Cletis), Norman Forsey

(Tersius), Kelson Henderson (Demicles), and Andrew Kovacevich (Sepsus)

When Lyla is killed by bigots who believe in "Athenian purity" and are against her marriage to Deric, the centaur, they burn down the couple's home. Lyla, after ordering her son to flee into the woods, is killed in the fire, and Deric seeks vengeance. The arriving Hercules and Salmoneus attempt to help out in the situation while stopping Deric from going too far. In the end, the child is discovered alive, and Hercules pleads with Zeus to restore Lyla to life.

Behind the Scenes "I guess if anybody did shows that were socially conscious, Bob Bielak did," John Schulian smiles. "The centaurs were always a marvel. Just that we could pull them off was amazing. Just to shoot them was difficult. They required a lot of blue screen shooting and were a logistic and production nightmare."

The episode also drove home the point that in *Hercules* nobody has to stay dead, as Zeus resurrected Lyla. "That was a fight with the studio that we lost," Schulian says. "We wanted her to be dead at the end, but the studio thought that it was too much of a downer. It's interesting that the show *Hercules* has a very light tone, overall, and *Xena* is a much darker show, even though people in the business treat it as if it's frothy. *Xena*'s a very dark show, much more what Rob Tapert would like to do.

"The kid we cast, James Croft, was the cutest kid I've ever seen in my life, and he had the attention span of a cabbage. When you're trying to shoot him, it's just impossible. He'd be there in a scene with one little thing to do, and he'd just be looking off somewhere. The dailies were even funny."

For his part, Bielak adds, "The casting of Lucy Lawless as Lyla was something of an embarrassment for the studio because they kind of knew at that time she was going to show up as Xena [on the spin-off], yet we wanted to tell this story. The centaurs are the third-world people of the ancient world, and we tend to use them for allegories in 'Outcast,' and we did that later with 'Centaur Mentor Journey.' This was our episode about prejudice and how people don't want to accept others who are different. It was a chance for Hercules to get up on his step stool, and at the same time it was the old posse-is-after-him chase.

"But the embarrassing thing for the studio," elaborates Bielak, "was that in the original script you never saw her face. I went to great lengths to say that Lyla was there, but she was in shadow or something, so they could have shot it with anybody. The main thing was that she died, the kid got away, then Hercules had to go and take this guy out of the realm of revenge. I don't know who changed it around first, but they wanted to actually see that it was Lucy, that we couldn't cast somebody else as the character. Even so, I still did it in such a way that she was in shadow, but eventually it came down to the end when the studio wanted her resurrected. We really fought that because we felt that it undermined the whole series. I think what it does to the audience after you do it a couple of times is that you don't feel that anyone is going to die; Herc is just going to bring them back to life. All I could do in those situations is raise my voice of protest, but once I'm heard it's my duty to shut up and go along. If I had been co-executive producer at the time, I maybe could have made a bigger stink. You know, they did it there, they brought Iolaus back to life, and I just think that kind of thing is a mistake. Dead is dead, and that's the end of it. Anyway, this is a mandate that came down from the Tower, that we couldn't kill somebody—a mother, for God's sake—in the teaser. But this is what it's all about. The wrong people die, but the kid has still got a father to take care of him. This is what our episode is about, this is where prejudice gets you. 'No, no, you've got to bring her back.' So we brought her back, and five minutes later Lyla shows up as Xena. By the time it dawned on them, it was too late, and it kind of came back to bite them in the ass. I got some satisfaction out of that."

Episode #19: "Under the Broken Sky"

Written by John Schulian
Directed by Jim Contner
Guest Starring Robert Trebor (Salmoneus), Bruce Phillips (Atticus), Carl Bland (Pilot), Maria Rangel (Lucina), Julie Collis (Heliotrope), Katherine Ransom

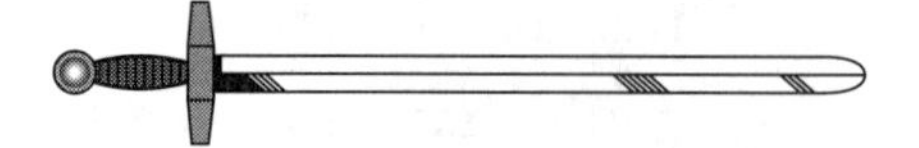

"What is the cost of being a hero? We keep coming back to that to lend a little juice to it. Kevin can give us that angst and give us that perspective of, 'Being a hero is nice on one hand, but there's a cost to it.'"

—Co-executive Producer Robert Bielak

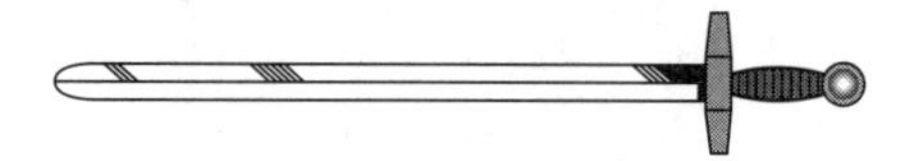

(Mica), John Mellor (Crossbow), Crawford Thorson (Thug), Jim Ngaata (Guard), Jean Hyland (Mother), Christine Bartlett (First Villager), Veronica Aalhurst (Second Villager), Daniel Batten (Weasel), and Grant Boccher (Customer)

While working in a pleasure palace, Salmoneus attempts to help a man who has been robbed by thieves employed by Pilot, who has been using his henchman to rule over Enola. Hercules arrives, warning Pilot that his days are numbered in this village. Things get a little more complicated when a woman named Lucina, employed as a dancer at the palace in an attempt to escape the guilt she feels for losing her children to illness, is approached sexually by Pilot. Her husband, Atticus, attacks the man but is stabbed for his troubles. Hercules—after having to save Salmoneus from Pilot's men—takes the couple to safety and turns his sights to Pilot.

Behind the Scenes John Schulian says, "A lot of this got shot on a soundstage. I really thought the action didn't work very well because of where we shot it. We used a director, Jim Contner, who was a really good director. He did *Wiseguy* and *Midnight Caller* and was a DP on *Crime Story,* and he was really very good. When he shot this, it was raining a lot down there, and we wound up working on the stage. The action sequences, one in particular, don't really work. But, I felt we got a very nice performance from the woman who played Lucina, Maria Rangel. She plays a woman who loses her two children to an epidemic of fever, and she feels that she is responsible. She's brokenhearted and runs off and becomes a prostitute. That's where we find her in the opening sequence. Jim Contner did a really nice sequence. The show opens with her dancing, and there's an overhead shot, and it really looks smashing. She really did a terrific job for us.

"Of course this story line got me into another big fight with the studio. They just thought it was too dark and too dicey. My feeling was—what it was is her husband comes after her and tries to bring her back home. Hercules helps get them together. It was a story that I really liked a lot. You can't do them all goofy, and when you say it's serious if you compare it to *ER* or *Homicide,* it's nothing. But the studio freaked over the fact that this woman had become a prostitute. On this one I held my ground once again, and we got it shot. I also thought the character of Pilot was just wonderful. He amused the hell out of me."

Episode #20: "The Mother of All Monsters"

Written by John Schulian
Directed by Bruce Seth Green
Guest Starring Bridget Hoffman (Echidna), Liddy Holloway (Alcmene), Martin Kove (Demetrius), Graham Smith (Leukos), Rebecca Clark (Archer Number One), Katrina Misa (Archer Number Two), Ian Miller (Chief Highwayman), Don Linden (Master of Ceremonies), Jack Dacey (Trapper), Peter Mason (Owner), and Colin Francis (Second Thief)

The various creatures Hercules has confronted and defeated through the course of the series must have come from *somewhere*—and in this episode we learn exactly where that is. A creature named Echidna is, quite literally, the mother of all monsters, and she has been pained deeply by the deaths of her offspring. Seeking vengeance, she hatches a plan to get retribution from Hercules by having one of her soldiers, Demetrius, seduce and capture

Hercules' mother, Alcmene, so that she can kill her. Hercules, aided by Iolaus, must face daunting challenges to retrieve his mother before it's too late.

Behind the Scenes Reflects John Schulian, "When you hear the actress's screeching voice, that's really the actress. It turned out to be a very good episode. There's some real nice stuff in it. As I recall, we open it up, and Hercules says he hasn't seen his mother for a while and he goes home. What appealed to me was the idea of a misunderstood monster: a mother whose children are twisted into doing evil things."

Despite the fact that the episode establishes that the creatures Hercules has battled are the offspring of Echidna, it had little influence on the writers in future episodes dealing with other monsters. "It may have occurred to somebody else, but it never occurred to me," he says. "I just sort of play them one at a time, so that didn't weigh on me."

Episode #21: "The Other Side"

Written by Robert Bielak
Directed by George Mendeluk
Guest Starring Tawny Kitaen (Deianeira), Andrea Croton (Persephone), Eric Thompson (Hades), Sarah Wilson (Demeter), Michael Hurst (Charon), David Banter (Tartalus), Simon Lewthwaite (Klonus), Paul McIver (Aeson), Rose McIver (Ilea), and Geoff Allen (Farmer)

Hercules finds himself in a quandary when Hades kidnaps the goddess Demeter's daughter, Persephone, and takes her to the underworld. Demeter wants Herc to retrieve her daughter, but he responds that matters between gods are not his concern. His attitude changes, however, when Demeter unleashes savage storms on Earth's surface. With little choice, Hercules crosses the River Styx, where he is briefly reunited with his dead wife and children, goes through the traditional battles to get to his goal, and is surprised to learn that the woman is not in such a rush to return to the surface.

Behind the Scenes "A great episode," enthuses John Schulian, "about the creation of the seasons, and Hercules goes to the other side to battle Hades for the girl, Persephone. Hercules crosses the River Styx, and the boatman, who's all tricked up, is

Michael Hurst, who normally plays Iolaus. He's very good and convincing as another character. Interesting for Hercules is that while he's on the other side he sees his family and is briefly reunited. I have to tell you, on shows of this tenor that we tried to do, this was far and away the most successful. I thought this was a really big episode. For me, Bob Bielak did consistently good work, but I thought this was him at his best.

"Kevin was really good in this, in a different way than you normally think of him being good," he adds. "It was about emotion, and he really came through. Just like in 'The Mother of All Monsters' when he goes back and visits his family's graves. Kevin could really find something inside himself where you could see the emotion; he could manufacture tears in a scene like that, and you didn't feel they were false. It's something that really good actors are able to do. With all due respect to Kevin, I don't think you would call him a real good actor, but he has that capacity, and he's very believable. I think that showing that sort of emotion and vulnerability makes him that much more appealing. Because here is the son of Zeus, he's the strongest guy in the world, he can kick everybody's ass, and yet he really feels. I think that's a really wonderful quality. In my tenure on *Hercules,* there wasn't one scene like that that he let us down in. Those moments absolutely add emotional resonance to the show. At the end of this episode Hercules has that choice: He can stay with his family or go back to Earth. He takes that last look at them and goes back home. That was really the one episode that I was involved in that worked in every way."

Offers Robert Bielak, "I think my two favorite episodes I wrote might very well be 'The Other Side' and 'Highway to Hades.' One of the reasons I like 'The Other Side' is that it really is one of our most mythological episodes. We really deal with Hades and Persephone there, though we did our own twist on the 'real' mythology. I think originally it was Zeus who decided that she would spend six months above and six months below, but that would have left Hercules with very little to do. There was actually a lot more humor in that episode that got cut out partially in the final script and mostly in the shooting. There was a whole substory about a pig farmer who was a much bigger part of the piece. He was out there with his pigs when this abduction took place, and they took his favorite pig as well. Besides trying to save Persephone, Hercules had to try and save the pig and bring that back. There was a whole little funny thing going on with that. That's the problem with TV—when you're trying to cut down on time, the first thing that goes is the humor and character moments. Invariably that's why the scripts are usually better than the show that ends up on the air. No matter how good the show is, the script probably was better because it had more of the grace notes and humor and all of the stuff that they couldn't fit in because of time constraints.

"I thought it was a good tale of love," he continues. "Some nice twists in it. We think that this girl has been abducted but, lo and behold, she *wants* to be with this guy. Hercules doesn't want to get involved with the gods, he's there to help mankind, and Demeter gives the Earth a perpetual winter unless he goes. It was also the first time we went to the other side, and it was a very dangerous, ballsy thing for him to do to go down there, not knowing if he's going to be able to come back. There was a lot of heart with the wife and kids, and he had his dilemma about them. It's all on the table, and he decides to continue in the job he signed on for."

Episode #22: "The Fire Down Below"

Written by Scott Smith Miller and John Schulian

Directed by Timothy Bond

Guest Starring Robert Trebor (Salmoneus), Stephanie Wilkin (Ayora), Stephen Hall (Purces), Teresa Hill (Nemesis), Andy Anderson (Zandar), Emma Menzies (Syreeta), Daniel Batten (Pyro), Geoff Clendon (Vormann), Roger Goodburn (Promoter), Mark Nua (Wrestler), Jon Brazier (Slave Trader), Jeff Gane (Peddler), Mary Henderson (Kundin), and James Marcum (Barkeeper)

Ever the treasure seeker, Salmoneus, working for a man named Zandar, has struck it rich when he comes across a hidden treasure. Unfortunately, this wealth was actually a gift from Hera to King Ores, and now all hell has broken loose, with both Hera and Nemesis, the Goddess of Retribution, striking out. While Hercules is able to convince Nemesis that Salmoneus was merely a puppet for Zandar, Hera, naturally, takes Zandar's side and equips him with a fire being known as Pyro to combat Hercules.

Behind the Scenes "Salmoneus rears his ugly head again," laughs John Schulian. "What I remember most about this episode is the special effects and the fire monster. I don't know if this was the toughest special effect they ever tried to do, but it was right up there. I thought it was great, yet I know they were never happy with it. They were always saying they could do better if they had one more week, one more day, one more hour. But I thought it was quite smashing. One of those things that not a lot of TV shows were doing; it's movie stuff."

Schulian points out that there are many difficulties having the writing staff in Los Angeles with the show's physical production taking place in New Zealand, among them being a loss of control once the script gets into the hands of the director. He points to this episode's helmer, Timothy Bond, as an example.

"Timothy Bond should be shot, as far as I'm concerned," he states candidly. "He took a script of mine and just trashed it. It drives home the problems of the long distance because a lot of these guys—the ones that come to mind are Bond and T.J. Scott—got down there, and they ran amok and did what they wanted to do and didn't pay the sort of attention to scripts that the other directors did. We were really at a disadvantage, and there were times when I felt our line producer, Eric Gruendemann, should have protected the script. I believe that was his job and felt that he didn't do it. I thought Eric was a very good line producer who was dealing with both *Hercules* and *Xena,* and he obviously had his hands full, but Tim Bond just completely betrayed us."

Episode #23: "Cast a Giant Shadow"

Written by John Schulian
Directed by John T. Kretschmer

Guest Starring Bridget Hoffman (Echidna), Glenn Shadix (Typhon), Stig Eldred (Maceus), Fiona Mogridge (Breanna), Bruce Hopkins (Pylon), Bruce Allpress (Septus), Bernard Moodi (Proprietor), and Steve Hall (Warrior)

Hercules frees the gentle giant Typhon from a curse placed on him by Hera, which makes her less than happy, and at the same time he must deal with the vengeance-seeking Maceus, whose brother, Demetrius, Herc killed in an earlier battle. Things go from bad to worse, though, when Hercules learns that Typhon is actually married to Echnida—the so-called Mother of All Monsters—and that the creatures he killed in earlier battles were actually their offspring. Maceus, who learns this as well, tries to turn Typhon against Hercules, but the giant ultimately comes to the conclusion that it was Hera who made his children evil. Later, when he's reunited with Echnida, he realizes that it has been Hera all along who has kept him apart from his wife. As a result, the couple realize that Herc is a better friend than an enemy.

Behind the Scenes "This is where we get to meet Echnida's husband, Typhon, played by Glenn Shadix, who is so wonderful and funny," says John Schulian. "I've got to tell you, Glenn was one of the true delights of the *Hercules* experience for me because we had a hard time casting this. We wanted somebody who has a real sweetness and innocence yet is a big guy. We had a huge casting session, and I think it was our casting director who really championed Glenn and got us to believe in him. There's a lot of subtext to this episode, with events of the past essentially catching up to the present. Everything you do has some sort of consequence, some sort of impact."

Episode #24: "Highway to Hades"

Written by Robert Bielak

Directed by T.J. Scott

Guest Starring Eric Thomson (Hades), Leslie Wing (Celeste), Ray Henwood (King Sisyphus), Craig Hall (Timuron), Angela Gribben (Daphne), Michael Hurst (Charon), Tony Wood (Eluvius), Ronald Hendricks (Epicurus), Barry Te Hora (Chief), Jane Cresswell (Maid), Megan Edwards (Servant), Tim Raby (Soldier), and David Mackie (Guard)

In a surprising turn of events, Hades actually comes to Hercules in search of a favor, explaining that King Sisyphus was destined to come to the underworld but worked it out that a man named Timeron unwittingly took his place. Now Hercules and Iolaus have three days to retrieve Sisyphus while at the same time allowing Timeron time with his wife—to whom he had been married only four hours at the time of his death—before his spirit passes over the Elysian Fields.

Behind the Scenes "This story sprang mostly from Rob Tapert," says Robert Bielak. "I was looking for a story and he said, 'Here are three kind of stories I want to do.' One of them was Hercules has to help three people who are heading to the underworld by mistake. I'm not even sure how it connected with the rest, but I was fighting with the idea, and one day I was in the shower and I saw these horses blowing smoke and fire out of their nostrils, charging through the dark, pulling this chariot. From there it all kind of fell into place. Who's driving the chariot? Hades. Why? He's looking for Hercules. It kind of all unfolded naturally.

"The other thing I like about this episode is that the villains have a point of view; they're at least truly motivated by something. There were a couple of nice reveals, which turned on their head the expectations some people might have had. The love story I thought worked. The truth is we borrow from so many different things and mix it all together, and when it works it's great. There were elements of *Ghost* in the episode where this couple never consummated their marriage. How are they going to do it? The rule is he was out for twenty-four hours and he can't go back. Well, use Hercules. You know, 'You want your spirit to occupy my body?' But it was nice. Again, it was well directed. It could have been smarmy and fallen flat.

"I think the early episodes gave me the chance to get that sort of bent humor out there that I didn't really get a chance to get out in a lot of other stuff that I've done. I've done *Scarecrow and Mrs. King, Tour of Duty, In the Heat of the Night,* and just a ton of shows, but there was something about *Hercules*' humor. I didn't have to edit myself, which was great. Besides that, I think there was a chance to get out personal philosophies without really getting up on a soapbox and boring people. For instance, the suicide thing with the girl in this episode, I think most people have been at the spot where they've asked themselves, 'Why go on?' My philosophy is it's going to come someday, why rush it? Why not stick around and see if things change? It's all cyclic. If it's bad today, it will probably get better tomorrow."

Episode #25: "The Sword of Veracity"

Written by Steven Baum
Directed by Garth Maxwell
Guest Starring Kim Michaels (Leah), Brad Carpenter (Amphion), Paul Minifie (Trachis), Danny Lineham (Lycus), Kelly Greene (Epius), Brendolan Lovegrove (Man), Anton Bentley (Head Guard), Amanda Rees (Mina), Michael Saccente (Talius), Anthony Ray Parker (Minotaur), and Shane Dawson (Second Minotaur)

When an innocent man, Amphion, is accused of a murder that he did not commit, Hercules and Iolaus must retrieve the Sword of Veracity to prove his innocence. The problem is that the sword, along with hundreds of others, is in a cave guarded by a minotaur, and Hercules must try each and every sword until he finds the right one so that Amphion will be set free and the guilty man brought to justice.

Behind the Scenes Admits John Schulian, "Not a very good episode. The first two acts, as I recall, were incredibly slow. A show like *Hercules* had a rhythm, and you really had to get into it in a hurry; you had to get things popping. This episode kind of unfolded at a leisurely pace. I'm sure we worked on it, but the format of a teaser and four acts is sometimes difficult. I don't have anything specific on it. I know we didn't get a very good performance out of our damsel in distress in this episode."

Episode #26: "The Enforcer"

Written by Nelson Costello
Directed by T.J. Scott
Guest Starring Teresa Hill (Nemesis), Karen Shepard (Enforcer), Jed Brophy (Gnatius), Andrew Kovacevich (Proprietor), Grant

Bochner (Hunter), Geoff Snell (Clytus), Paula Keenan (Drunkard), Toni Marsch (First Maid), Asa Lindh (Second Maid), Jeff Gane (Gang Boss), Adrian Keeling (First Man), and Ross Harper (Second Man)

In a battle with Hera, Nemesis is stripped of her powers, and she turns to Hercules for help in adapting to life as a mortal. Nothing is easy when Hera's involved, however, and the duo find themselves going up against a female warrior born from the waters of this planet—who literally splatters apart during battle and then pulls herself back together—and a deadly enforcer.

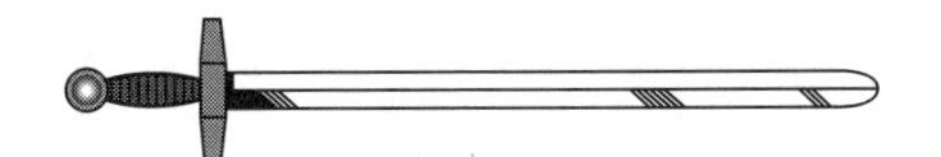

"[Lucy Lawless] played the part. I saw the first day's dailies and she's riding a horse, swinging a sword and kicking the crap out of people—well, there's Xena. Had no idea that it would go on to become the phenomenon that it has become."

—Co-executive Producer John Schulian on "The Warrior Princess"

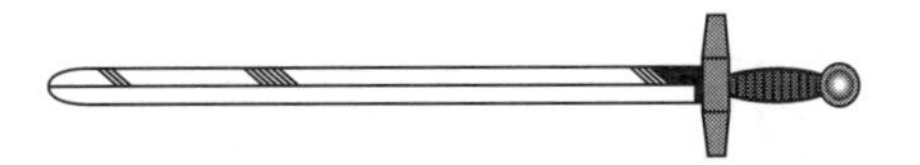

Behind the Scenes "Our *Terminator* episode," John Schulian smiles. "That was the format of the show, although we used a woman in the role. There's some very violent stuff that goes on in this show, which was directed by T.J. Scott. Although I spoke ill of him, he does have a real good flair for action. The fight between Hercules and the Enforcer has a much harder-edge quality to it. A lot of our fights have a certain gag quality to them where you're throwing guys through walls and stuff like that. This was more charged."

Episode #27: "Once a Hero"

Written by Robert Bielak and John Schulian
Directed by Robert Tapert
Guest Starring Jeffrey Thomas (Jason), Peter Feeney (Castor), Edward Campbell (Artemus), Anthony Ray Parker (Valerus), Tim Raby (Archivus), Willa O'Neill (Phoebe), John Sumner (Domesticles), Mark Nua (Otus), Latham Gaines (Marcus), Belinda Todd (Princess), Campbell Rousselle (Robber), and Paul Morell (Falafel)

Jason—as in Jason and the Argonauts—must pull himself out of a personal funk and reclaim the trust of his crew when the Golden Fleece is stolen by a demon warrior. Hercules joins them on their quest, helping the reunited crew as they take on this warrior, who turns out to be one of their own and now a member of Hera's followers, in order to retrieve the fleece. Their obstacles include an army of skeletons that move as though they're alive.

Behind the Scenes John Schulian explains, "This was basically an urban renewal of Jason's soul. This was the first episode Rob Tapert ever directed for us, so it was a big affair. Lots of action."

One sequence in particular—a battle with skeleton warriors—is apparently lifted conceptwise from the Ray Harryhausen film *Jason and the Argonauts.* "Rob Tapert is very influenced not only by Chinese action movies but also by the Harryhausen movies. Certainly these shows reflect those."

Explains Robert Bielak, "The making of this episode was a very strange situation. There were a lot of politics going on at that time, a lot of unhappiness. There was the arbitration between Robert Tapert and John Schulian over the creator credit for *Xena;* Rob was going through a lot of personal problems. John and I were writing this episode, did the story, did the first couple of passes on it. I can't remember how we split it up, but all of a sudden we found ourselves with another writer rewriting us. Ultimately it came back to John to do the polish on, but a bad taste was had by all. It was an episode that Rob directed, too, and I don't think it turned out quite as well as anybody wanted it to, although it did have a pretty good skeleton fight in there. I stood corrected on that, actually, because early on in the story I told everyone that I wasn't interested in seeing skeletons fight because they seem so fragile. What's the point? I think Rob wanted to do it as an homage to Harryhausen's version of *Jason and the Argonauts.* I think the effects came out better in ours than in that one. Again, going toward the audience we were aiming at mostly, we tried to encompass everyone. There's humor for adults and action for the early teenage boys. I think the action of the fighting skeletons was directed toward the young teenagers that would like it, and it turned out better than I thought it would. I stand corrected on my reservations.

"There were a number of problems," he says. "The character aspects of the characters never came out. You never really knew them. I think the episode that John and I had in mind was more of a relationship between Hercules and Jason and more of who Jason was. The basics remain the same—he was a guy who fell on hard times and became a drunk. Again, we follow fairly closely the mythological origins of it, which was that after Jason married Medea, he found a sweet young thing and threw Medea aside, and she got her revenge by burning up both the sweet young thing and Jason's kids. In our version, all of the guilt from that turned Jason into a drunk. He's still king, but not much of a king, and Hercules is acting like a catalyst to help this man find his redemption in the story. I think our version was a little richer with that background, with the relationship between them, with that whole redemption aspect. I think the draft that came in from the outsider shied away from that, went more toward action. When Rob shot it, I think he emphasized the action at the expense of the character, and when it came back long—again, you have to fit these things into forty-three minutes—the first thing to go was the humor and the character beats and nuances. Even he admits that there is more action in that episode than there really should be. It still turned out to be a decent episode, but we thought it could have been richer than it was."

Episode #28: "Heedless Hearts"

Written by Robert Bielak
Directed by Peter Ellis
Guest Starring Audie England (Rheanna), Michael Keir-Morrisey (Melkos), Michael Saccente (Grovelus), Nigel Godfrey (Syrus), Bruce Hopkins (Jordis), Grant Triplow (Clarion), Robert Hogwood (Vericles), Sara Wiseman (Hephates), and Doug McCallan (Guard)

Hercules begins to second-guess his decision to help a woman named Rheanna in her people's rebellion against their leader, King Melkos. It seems that Iolaus—who has been struck by lightning and now has prophetic flashes of events in the future—has foreseen that Rheanna is planning on betraying Hercules. His dilemma is that he has started to fall in love with her and is torn between what he should and should not do.

Behind the Scenes "A decent episode, it should have been stronger," admits Robert Bielak. "I don't know if it went back to my writing or if it was the directing. I know part of it was the directing in the sense that there were one or two moments in the piece that should have been *really* big moments of Hercules with this lady. This was kind of a *Casablanca*-type story, with Hercules falling for the girl. They think the husband is dead, they think they've got a future together, and bam, the husband comes back to life. There should have been a couple of big moments where you said, 'Oh, Herc is finally getting over losing his wife and kids, and he's finally got a chance for happiness. Here's a girl he loves, and she loves him.' It was underwritten, and purposely so. I was trying to avoid the clichés and trying not to hit things on the head too hard. Sometimes that's a mistake in TV because you do things so fast that, depending on the director you get, sometimes it's better to lay it all out there and make sure you get the message across and not rely on the director building those messages. I think in TV more so than film—that's why one lapses into cliché and the shortcuts and all that, because you only have the forty-three minutes and you're still trying to get the emotions across and what's going on between these people. In a sense, I may have made a mistake by erring on the subtle side and the director missed it. There was one scene specifically that in dailies I took exception to. It was thrown away, and I think I even wrote it in the stage direction that even though the dialogue was very sparse, there was supposed to be a look that conveyed everything. The director kind of went right by it, and you missed the emotional resonance between these two people. Once you miss that, the ending kind of falls apart too. It's not such a tragedy when he has to give her up."

Episode #29: "Let the Games Begin"

Written by John Schulian
Directed by Gus Trikonis
Guest Starring Robert Trebor (Salmoneus), Cory Everson (Atalanta), Matthew Humphrey (Damon), Paul Glover (Brontus), Chris Bailey (Tarkon), John Watson (Taphius), Jason Honte (Lieutenant), Marcus Ponton (Soldier), Chris McKibbin (Chief), Norman Palacid (Salesman), Brenda Kendall (Customer), Morgan Palmer-Hubbard (First Boy), and Timothy Dale (Second Boy)

When the Eleans and the Spartans are on the verge of all-out war in their claims that each is more powerful than the other, Hercules intercedes and suggests that they try to prove themselves as sportsmen, partaking in what must be the world's first Olympics. Salmoneus is there to make a buck, as always, accompanied by less than honest participants, who are willing to try and win no matter what it takes.

Behind the Scenes "Atalanta makes a return appearance," says John Schulian, "and this is the episode where Cory Everson made such a terrific improvement actingwise. She notched it up and was really funny in it. She was still that body-brawling kind of babe but was funny and just had a nice repartee going with Kevin. I thought the two of them together were a lot of fun. I really admired the way she had improved. I don't know if it was just seeing what she had done in 'Ares' or if she had taken acting lessons or what, but she was great. This was about Herc starting the Olympics. You didn't know that, did you? It was an

Olympic year when we made the episode, and that served as the impetus for the story."

Episode #30: "The Apple"

Written by Steven Baum
Directed by Kevin Sorbo
Guest Starring Alexandra Tydings (Aphrodite), Rhonda McHardy (Artemis), Amanda Lister (Athena), Claire Yarlett (Thera), Jonathan Black (Epius), Ian Mune (King Sidon), Stephen Tozer (Diadorus), John Smith (Socrates), Peter Needham (Plato), Sam Williams (Comrade), and Vicky Barrett (Old Woman)

Iolaus finds himself in the seemingly enviable position of having to decide who—among the goddesses Aphrodite, Artemis, and Athena—is the most beautiful. As if this wasn't bad enough, Aphrodite also casts a spell that makes Iolaus desirable to Princess Thera, which could have serious ramifications on her people as well as those of her fiancé, Prince Epius. Hercules, who has been trying to enjoy some time "off," has to make sense out of this mess and straighten things out before things get too out of hand.

Behind the Scenes "This is the debut of Aphrodite, the goddess of love," muses John Schulian. "Our surfer girl. Steven Baum's first episode was pretty ordinary for us, but he really struck on something quite wonderful in coming up with Aphrodite, and he did make her a surfer/valley girl. It really works. One of the things we tried to do in *Hercules* is that we wanted the dialogue to be contemporary but didn't want anyone to say, 'Yo, dude.' That was the line you could not cross. But this just worked so well, and we got this actress, Alexandra Tydings, to play Aphrodite. I don't know what she's capable of beyond it, but she was absolutely perfect in this role. She was funny and is a great looking woman. This episode was one of the really great, fun episodes in my tenure on *Hercules.*

"As director," he elaborates, "I thought Kevin Sorbo did a fine, workmanlike job. I remember he shot a sequence to start the episode, some artsy sequence, and we had to cut it because the episode was running too long and that was the most expendable thing. He was very bent out of shape about that, but it was simple necessity. Welcome to the wonderful world of TV directing."

Episode #31: "The Promise"

Written by Michael Marks
Directed by Stewart Main
Guest Starring Marton Csokas (Tarlus), Joel Tobeck (King Beraeus), Josephine Davison (Ramina), Calvin Tutead (Natras), Michael Robinson (Lieutenant), Paul Norell (Falafel), Lee-Jane Foreman (Servant), and Matthew Sunderland (Shepherd)

When his soon-to-be-wife is kidnapped, King Beraeus turns to Hercules and Iolaus for help. The duo are more than happy to lend a hand but are at a loss when they learn that this woman, Romina, is actually in love with the man who supposedly kidnapped her.

Episode #32: "King for a Day"

Written by Patricia Manney
Directed by Anson Williams
Guest Starring Brendan Lovegrove (Pylon), Derek Payne (Hector), Ross McKellar (Lisos), Max Cryer (Priest), Zo Hartley (Tenant), Tim Hosking (Host), Brendan Perkins (Attica Guard), Tony Williams (Farmer), Matthew Jeffs (First Guard), John Ron Kempt (Second Guard), Tim Biggs (Farmer), Michael Bajko (Husband), Johanna Elms (Daughter), and Matt Elliott (Whimpering Lackey)

Although they always looked similar to each other, Iolaus is shocked to discover that his cousin, Prince Orestes, now is a dead ringer for him. This takes on special meaning when the Prince is drugged by his brother and Iolaus is asked to take his place for political reasons and for fear that Orestes would botch things up politically. Ironically, Iolaus becomes the kind of leader that the people want, which means that Orestes, once he's ready to take his own place, must make some changes for the sake of his subjects and the woman he loves, who is falling in love with Iolaus/Orestes.

Behind the Scenes John Schulian observes, "This is what we call one of our 'Hercules Lite' episodes in which Kevin, when I believe we shot it, had to come back to the States for something, and we basically shot the episode with Hercules in the first and last scenes, which were really uncomplicated. The idea is that Kevin could do those in half a day and be gone. Iolaus is a dead ringer for one of the many kings in ancient Greece, and he winds up saving the day.

"I'm sure there were X number of people out there who were disappointed that Kevin wasn't on screen, but I would bet that the older people who watch *Hercules,* eighteen and above, who were a little more sophisticated probably liked the episode a great deal because it was a lot of fun. I have no idea whether or not what I'm saying is right, but it's my feeling. Michael Hurst just picked up the ball and ran with it."

Episode #33: "Protean Challenge"

Written by Brian Herskowitz
Directed by Oley Sassone
Guest Starring Ashley Lawrence (Daniella), Jane Cresswell (Proteus), Paul Gittins (Thanius), James O'Farrell (Bornus), Stephen Papps (Tritos), John O'Leary (Magistrate), Alan Farquhar (First Villager), Tamar Howe (Second Villager), Lillian Enting (Old Woman), and Meredith Chalmers (Girl)

When Hercules and Iolaus attempt to clear their friend Thanus from the charge of robbery, they are eventually stunned to learn that there are doubles of all three of them making appearances in the village. Hercules eventually discovers that this is being caused by the god Proteus, who has the ability to change his form and is out to settle a score, using anyone he has to in order to do so. It culminates in a battle between Hercules and himself.

Behind the Scenes "Brian Herskowitz just understood the show infinitely better than just about any other freelancer that we had," John Schulian opines. "He walked in the door and just *got it.* He was able to come up with a real good story. I suppose in great moments in the legendary journeys of Hercules, the battle between the two Hercules' in this episode ranks right up there as one of the more bizarre sights."

Episode #34: "The Wedding of Alcmene"

Written by John Schulian
Directed by Timothy Bond
Guest Starring Jeffrey Thomas (Jason), Liddy Holloway (Alcmene), Sabrina Karsenti

(Sera), Nathaniel Lees (Blue Priest), Simon Prast (Patronius), Simone Kessell (Rena), and Kevin Smith (Iphicles)

Hercules is stunned to learn that Jason plans on wedding his mother, Alcmene, but Hera is pleased in that she can finally pinpoint where Hercules will be at a specific moment so that she can strike out at him. Waiting until the ceremony is taking place, she unleashes a sea creature that swallows up both Herc and Jason. Refusing to be digested quietly, they kill the creature from within and manage to escape when it washes ashore. The wedding takes place, with Hera failing yet again.

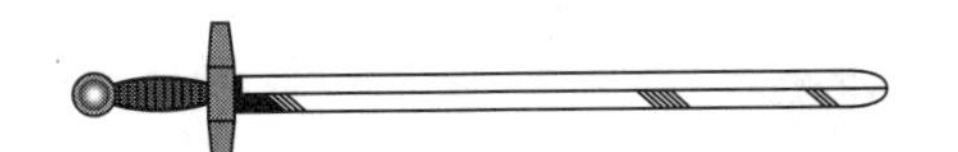

"Reb Brown [is] a handsome guy, and he's really put together, but he doesn't have a voice that goes with the rest of him. It's like what they say about pretty girls who can't act: God doesn't give with both hands."
—Co-executive Producer John Schulian on "The Vanishing Dead"

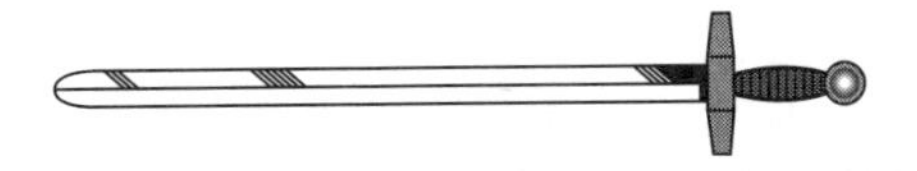

Behind the Scenes "The sea monster rears its ugly head," John Schulian notes. "What happened with this episode is that director Timothy Bond really made a strategical blunder by becoming so entranced with doing this sea monster that swallows Hercules and Jason. In my script, and the way the episode should have been shot, the monster consumes the last big action piece. We had seen it periodically throughout, as I recall. Tim Bond—I could see it happening before he left for New Zealand—kept coming up

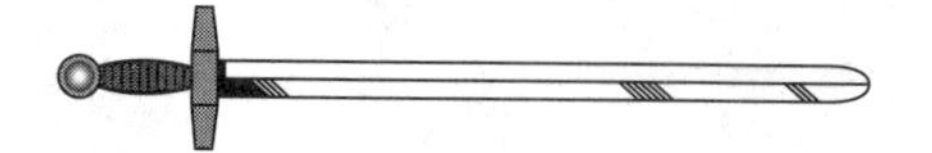

"Kevin Sorbo is really the rock on which all of these [shows] are built. He's a guy who can do the humor ... and he's surprisingly moving.... He really was the right guy to play Hercules. Without him the show would spin off its axis."

—Co-executive Producer John Schulian

with ways to handle the sea monster. I kept saying, 'Tim, you've got to shoot the episode, you can't let the monster eat the episode.' Well, that's what he did. When he got down there, to compensate for all the time he was devoting to the monster, he wound up combining other scenes, and he did it artlessly. The man is not a writer and not anything close to it, and Eric Gruendemann is completely at fault on this because one of his duties down there as line producer is to keep the directors in line. He didn't do it. I don't know who rewrote those scenes, but it was somebody who never had the guts to step forward. The episode really suffered because of that. The scenes were an embarrassment, and it remains an episode that the memory of which really angers me."

Episode #35: "The Power"

Written by Nelson Costello
Directed by Charlie Haskell
Guest Starring Robert Trebor (Salmoneus), Greer Robson (Siren), David Drew Gallagher (Dion), Bruce Phillips (Jucobus), Grant Bridger (Caris), Patrick Wilson (Old Titus), Liam Vincent (Young Titus), Greg Johnson (First Bandit), Christian Hodge (Second Bandit), Lulu Alach (Delia),

Mark Sinclair (Fisherman), Greg Norman (Fishmonger), William Lose (Tavern Owner), and Elaine Bracey (Villager)

A man named Dion, the son of Aphrodite, has the power to get people to follow what he says, and everyone around him is attempting to use that power for their own selfish purposes. Hercules steps in and does his best to make Dion aware of how he is being used. Hercules hopes that he will use these powers to benefit the world around him rather than a selfish few.

Episode #36: "Centaur Mentor Journey"

Written by Robert Bielak
Directed by Stephen L. Posey
Guest Starring Tony Blackett (Ceridian), Julian Arahanga (Cassius), James Townshend (Theseus), Marcia Cameron (Myrra), Mark Clare (Gnoxius), Edward Newborn (Perdiclis), John McKee (Gredor), Robert McMullen (Locus), Mark Clare (Grosius), Jonathan Bell-Booth (First Centaur), Ray Bishop (Second Centaur), John Freeman (Blacksmith), Lance Phillips (Rigis), and Fred Craig (Moog)

Civil tension between humans and centaurs is heating up, with one centaur in particular, Cassius, building an army of revolutionary creatures determined to force humanity to treat them as equals or die. War seems all but inevitable until Hercules intercedes and attempts to convince both sides of the need for racial tolerance.

Behind the Scenes "Kind of a strange episode," admits Robert Bielak, "and kind of a learning episode for me, I guess. We had boxed ourselves into a real corner with that. Again, we were back with the centaurs and doing social commentary on the oppressed centaurs. We had on one hand Martin Luther King and on the other side Malcolm X. I'm really not trying to trivialize here with that analogy, and I'm so afraid that it's going to come across that way. What you have on one side is the guy who taught Hercules, who's his mentor. Even though he taught him how to defend himself, martial arts and all that, his thrust is that there has to be peaceful means to get what you want. Up and coming is the young centaur who's saying, 'We've been doing that for years and years, and we haven't gotten anywhere, people won't let us drink at the water fountain in the town that we helped build. We have our rights, and if they won't respect us and give us our rights, we'll take them by force if necessary.' So into that comes Hercules, trying, again, to keep the peace and prevent the outbreak of violence between both sides, who have a legitimate tale to tell. All of these forces are coming together, and it's a tragedy that's about to erupt and that shouldn't happen.

"The problem with the episode in terms of *Hercules* is that the whole series is built on action, and the whole thrust of this episode is to go to a point of inaction. After we got into it and realized this is what Hercules has to stand for, we realized we had shackled ourselves. Here's this man of action who can't take action; his whole thing is to stop any kind of violence from happening. It became kind of an aberration for the series because usually we build to these fourth-act climaxes of kick ass, fight the monster, and get rid of the bad guys. In this one, it's almost anticlimactic because it turned into a march for peace and didn't quite have that drag-you-along-by-the-bootstraps or what's-going-to-happen feel to the end of the piece. That said, again I felt good about the episode. It wasn't as strong as some of the other ones. It wasn't like the first-season episodes I did where I really felt like I was on the top of my game, plus the way they turned out and were edited and directed. These fell into the middle level. Nothing to be ashamed of, but they could have been a little bit better.

"The joke around our place is that the centaur stories are the director killers," Bielak laughs. "I've done three centaur episodes, and after every one the director who has done it has never come back. It's because they're very hard. To do the effects right, you've got to shoot a scene with a horse being led by wires, then you have to shoot a man come in and be perfectly placed and do his lines and speak in the same place the horse was, then they've got to take care of that in special effects. It's very time consuming, it's all nuts and bolts stuff. It's not the fun of getting the performance out or the fun of the action, it's just nut and bolts, hard stuff to do.

So we lost director Stephen Posey after that one."

Episode #37: "Cave of Echoes"

Written by John Schulian and Robert Bielak
Directed by Gus Trikonis
Guest Starring Owen Black (Parenthesis), Mandy Gilette (Melina), Mark Perry (Elopius), and Grant McFarland (First Ruffian)

Hercules and Iolaus attempt to rescue a woman trapped in the so-called Cave of Echoes, in which voices literally boom back to their speakers. They are joined by a journalist named Parenthesis, a man of little self-esteem, fleeing soldiers who are after him for printing untruths. Because the man needs to have his confidence restored, Hercules details to him, through numerous flashbacks, some of the adventures he and Iolaus have experienced.

Behind the Scenes "'Cave of Echoes'? Did we do that?" Robert Bielak smiles facetiously. "The least of all our efforts culminated in the 'Cave of Echoes.' Once a year you have to do a bottle show. Fortunately we have a lot of caves in *Hercules*, but if it wasn't a cave it would have been an elevator on a detective show. You shoot on one location for four days, five days max, and it buys you time. You don't do any effects or any action, what you do is just have people yap away, and this is maybe where you do your clip show where you can rerun all the stuff you shot already. The reason to do it is to totally save money. At this time of the year you usually run out of your effects money, the action budget, and the whole thing, and you're looking for ways to save money no matter what. This culminates in either a clip show or a bottle show. This one was just sort of a shaggy dog tale: We did it as cheaply as possible, one setting—a cave—we had them wander around, followed around by this guy, and talk about their past experiences. It wasn't a great episode. It's rare when they do turn out okay. That being said, they're popular with the audience because it is a chance for them to catch up on the episodes that they missed, monsters they didn't see before, or revisit ones that they really like and want to see again. I wouldn't go so far as to call this show a work of art, but this episode is far down the rung on the ladder that is *Hercules*."

Groans John Schulian, "This was *really* bad. Bob and I bottomed out on this one. You have to do bottle shows, they become a financial necessity, but, lord, are you cheating your audience. Maybe shortchanging is a kinder word than cheating. I suppose there are guys who have done great bottle shows, but Bob and I aren't in their number. Let's let it go at that."

HERCULES: THE LEGENDARY JOURNEYS YEAR THREE (1996)

All Episodes 43 Minutes in Length

Production Credits

Executive Producers: Sam Raimi
Robert Tapert
Co-executive Producers: John Schulian
Robert Bielak
Jerry Patrick Brown
Co-producers: David Eick
Liz Friedman
Coordinating Producer: Bernadette Joyce
New Zealand Producer: Chloe Smith
Story Editor: Chris Manheim
Unit Production Manager: Chloe Smith
First Assistant Director: Paul Grinder
Second Assistant Director: Neal James
Director of Photography: Donald Duncan
Edited by: Jim Pryor
Visual Effects: Kevin O'Neill
Flat Earth Productions, Inc.
Production Designer: Robert Gillies
Costume Designer: Nigla Dickson
New Zealand Casting: Diana Rowan
Stunt Coordinator: Peter Bell

Regulars

Kevin Sorbo as Hercules
Michael Hurst as Iolaus/Charon

Semiregulars

Robert Trebor as Salmoneus
Bruce Campbell as Autolycus
Kevin Smith as Ares
Liddy Holloway as Alcmene

Episode #38: "Mercenary"

Written by Robert Bielak
Directed by Michael Hurst
Guest Starring Jeremy Roberts (Dirkus Patronicus/The Mercenary), Neil Duncan (Serfin), and Phil Jones (Trayan)

When the prison ship Enyalios begins to sink, Hercules sets free a mercenary he's been transporting so that the man will have a fair opportunity to survive this ordeal. They wash up on an island, where the prisoner knocks him out and escapes. Hercules sets off in pursuit, but when pirates come ashore in search of gold they believe was on the Enyalios, Hercules and the prisoner decide to work together, eluding the pirates and the man-eating sand rays

"The thing that interested me about this story line was creating a situation that had a moral dilemma for Hercules. If it was just a physical obstacle, we always knew he would overcome it because he's the strongest man on earth."

—Writer/Director Doug Lefler on "The King of Thieves"

that live in a desertlike area of the island.

Behind the Scenes "Actually I thought this episode turned out really well," offers Robert Bielak. "Although we did have monsters in it, it was a darker piece than the usual Hercules. It was, again, one of the times that we put Hercules out on the dilemma of what to do. Here's a guy who obviously has killed people, taken the law into his own hand and stuff, yet he's not going back to justice. What do you do in that situation? Along the way I think there was an interesting arc to the Dirkus character. When we meet him we think he's the worst guy in the world; here's a guy who after Hercules frees him from drowning, breaks his arm, and runs off anyway. What kind of jerk is that? But the more you unpeel the onion of this character, the more you see that he just has a different code. It's actually not such a bad code, it's just that it's a little outside the realm of legality and upholding the law the way Hercules does. As you move through the piece, you learn more and more about him, and I think Hercules learns more and more about him. It wasn't just black and white, this guy wasn't out to kill anybody; the people he killed probably deserved to die. It doesn't give him an excuse to take the law into his own hands, but the guy is not the black bastard that Hercules thought in the beginning. Eventually they do have to have some sort of bonding to get out of their predicament together. I thought it was a pretty well done, nicely shot, nicely acted episode.

"And Michael Hurst has turned into a really good director for us. He's just a very talented guy. He's probably the best actor in the series; he can do anything. Kevin is very good at the fastball-down-the-middle stuff, but he doesn't have the range that Michael does. He can do comedy, action, heavy drama, he can direct. He really adds a lot to the whole mix. I think early on he helped Kevin find himself and the character a little, too. Every time Kevin would have problems with certain lines or certain attitudes, Michael was there to show him where and how to do it. I think it's that Shakespearean background that the British seem to have in their best actors. New Zealanders and Australians come out of that, too, I think. They respect the word more. It's probably a misquote, but Olivier one time was rehearsing a play, and a young actor came up to him and said something like, 'These lines, I just can't make them work. I can't say them.' Olivier said in response, 'Well, I thought our job was to make them work.' That, I think, is the British attitude toward it, and it's an attitude that the best actors have. There's not enough time for every line to be golden in TV. That's an unfortunate fact of life—you have a limited time to get these things together. There's always rewriting that can be done on it, there's always more time taken for shooting, editing, and the whole thing. But there's just not that kind of time in TV. You do the best you can in the allotted time. But a lot of actors make it harder on themselves. Rather than trying to find a way to make the line work, they'll go through all kinds of machinations to come up with a different line and in doing so will change the piece because they've left out an important word or two that is a clue or is a character thing that reflects on

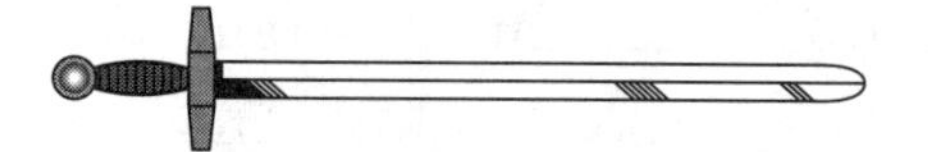

"The casting of Lucy Lawless as Lyla was something of an embarrassment for the studio because they kind of knew at that time she was going to show up as Xena [on the spin-off]."
—Co-executive Producer Robert Bielak on "Outcast"

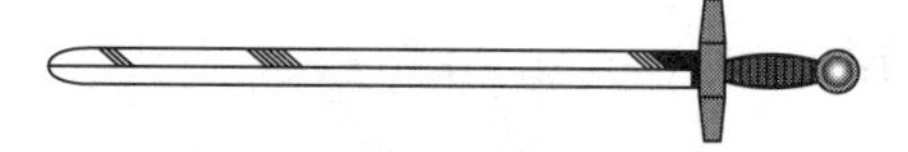

what's going to happen in act four. They don't always see the big picture. Truthfully, that hasn't been a big problem on this show. We've run into occasional things, but for the most part it comes back with at least the intent being right. My philosophy as a writer on TV is that there's a few lines in every script that I really love and don't want changed at all, but the other stuff services the plot, services the story. If you want to put it into your own words so that you can say it easier, as long as it doesn't affect the outcome or the character or what's happening down the line, feel free. I know Bochco would probably die hearing that. That's his prerogative, too. I'm not in that class of writer, and if I had Bochco's talent, maybe I'd feel the same way. I feel that I'm a good journeyman writer who can do almost anything, but I'm not in that art quality."

Interjects John Schulian, "Not the world's greatest episode, but it wound up working in some odd way. If somebody ever names their top ten *Hercules* episodes, I don't think it will ever be there, but it worked alright."

Episode #39: "Doomsday"

Written by Brian Herskowitz
Directed by James Whitmore, Jr.
Guest Starring Derek Payne (Daedalus), Franke Stevens (King Nikolos), and Fiona Mogridge (Moria)

Grieving over the death of his son, Icarus, an emotionally defeated Daedalus offers his inventions to the evil King Nikolos, including a suit of body armor that makes its wearer more powerful than even Hercules. This is nearly proven in a battle with Herc, when he arrives in this village, accompanied by a female journalist named Moria. In the end, and after seeing the harm that has come to Hercules, Daedalus realizes that he is dishonoring his son's memory.

Episode #40: "Love Takes a Holiday"

Written by Gene O'Neill and Noreen Tobin
Directed by Charlie Haskell
Guest Starring Alexandra Tydings (Aphrodite), Sarah Smuts-Kennedy (Leandra), Julian Garnder (Hephaestus), Mervyn Smith (Iagos), and Fiona Mogridge (Evanthea)

A disillusioned Aphrodite quits her day job as the goddess of love, and relationships all over the planet fall into ruin. Iolaus decides to take matters into his own hands, discovering the source of Aphrodite's unhappiness and doing what he can to convince her that she can still love.

Episode #41: "Mummy Dearest"

Written by Melissa Rosenberg
Directed by Anson Williams
Guest Starring Robert Trebor (Salmoneus), Galyn Gorg (Anuket), John Watson (Sokar), Henry Vaeoso (Keb), Mark Newnham (Mummy), Alan De Malmanche (Phineus), David Stott (Thief Number One), and Derek Ward (Thief Number Two)

Salmoneus, as usual, causes trouble when he decides to open a "House of Horrors," using an actual Egyptian mummy he's purchased from a pair of grave robbers. This mummy—thanks to Salmoneus removing an ankh from around its neck—comes back to life, and it is up to Hercules to undo the damage and stop something that is already dead.

Behind the Scenes Says John Schulian, "We were probably bending the rules a little bit in terms of combining Hercules with a mummy, but Melissa Rosenberg [the episode's writer] was a good sport about it. The amazing thing to me about *Hercules* is the way that the various episodes are up and down and all over the place. Some of the episodes should never have hit the airwaves. Despite the constantly changing quality of the various episodes, the show definitely filled a void. People were really looking for something like this show."

Episode #42: "Not Fade Away"

Written by John Schulian
Directed by T.J. Scott
Guest Starring Cynthia Rothrock (Enforcer Number Two), Karen Shepard (Enforcer Number One), Liddy Holloway (Alcmene), Jeffrey Thomas (Jason), Bruce Allpress (Skouros), Erik Thomson (Hades), Andrea Croton (Persephone), Gordon Hatfield (Freedom Fighter), and Geoff Clendon (Witness)

When Hercules and Iolaus witness Hera's lightning strike on the village of Thebes, Hercules reflects on the death of his family and sets off to proceed to their gravesites. Hera's second enforcer attacks Iolaus to find out where Hercules is, nearly killing the man in the process. Iolaus makes it to Hercules, tells him what has happened, and then dies. Devastated, Hercules brings Iolaus to Hades and asks him to return the mortal to life in repayment for what Herc did for the underworld ruler with Persephone. Hades agrees, although he does have some conditions that Hercules must meet.

Behind the Scenes "The title of this episode came from an old Buddy Holly song," John Schulian reveals. "The 'enforcer' comes back because there's a worse enforcer out there. In other words, this is our take on *Terminator 2*. This one is just big action, brawling stuff with Cynthia Rothrock and Karen Shepard. They're two heavy-duty female movie martial artists. This one, which may or may not be the greatest thing made artistically, was significant in that we were able to get a couple of B-movie stars in a TV series. This is just full speed ahead, let's see how many headlights we can break."

Episode #43: "Monster-Child in the Promised Land"

Written by John Schulian
Directed by John T. Kretchmer
Guest Starring Bridget Hoffman (Echidna), Glenn Shadix (Typhon), Grant Heslov (Klepto), Tony Wood (Bluth), Rebecca Clark (Header Archer), Bernard Woody

(Messenger), and Jane Bishop (Elderly Woman)

When a thief named Klepto steals the newest child of Echidna and Typhon to sell on the black market, Hercules and Iolaus become determined to retrieve the child and bring the thief to justice. Echidna, fearful that yet another of her children will be turned against people rather than loving all living things, is fearful she will never get the child back. Actually helping the duo in their quest is the fact that Klepto, who had connected emotionally with the child before selling him, is so remorseful that he will do anything he can to help.

Behind the Scenes "This was our little heartwarming Hercules-saving-the-baby episode," says John Schulian. "Actually it's really about the baby and Klepto, and everybody else is standing around, hanging on for dear life. Probably not an episode that's among Kevin's favorites because the focus really isn't on him. I should have known better as the writer, but I just fell in love with the characters. Actually, when I wrote this we were hoping that Pee Wee Herman, Paul Reubens, would play the role, but we couldn't work it out. Looking back at the *Hercules* episodes, I think I like this one a lot, as well as 'Mother of All Monsters' and 'Eye of the Beholder,' as well as the so-called Xena trilogy."

Episode #44: "The Green-Eyed Monster"

Written by Steven Baum
Directed by Chuck Braverman
Guest Starring Robert Trebor (Salmoneus), Alexandra Tydings (Aphrodite), Karl Urban (Cupid), Susan Word (Psyche), Patrick Brenton (Satyr Number One), Mike Howell (Pelops), and Simon Gomez (Saltar)

What happens when Cupid himself is smitten? All kind of chaos ensues, and, in answer to a request from Aphrodite, Hercules becomes involved in the sometimes volatile relationship between Cupid and the woman Psyche, who all men seem attracted to.

Behind the Scenes "A terrific episode," says John Schulian. "Alexandra Tydings rides again. Aphrodite is ageless, so you have some guy calling her mom. Just the thought of that sets the tone for the whole episode; she just doesn't want to admit that she could have a kid who is of marrying age, and she wants to break up the wedding because she's threatened. She's facing her own mortality here. Think of a great-looking woman who had a child at age eighteen, and now she's forty and she's got a twenty-two-year-old son or daughter getting married. She probably still looks great, and it's that kind of mindset. It was a charming and funny episode."

Episode #45: "Prince Hercules"

Teleplay by Robert Bielak
Story by Brad Carpenter
Directed by Charles Siebert
Guest Starring Jane Thomas (Queen Parnassa), Paul Gittins (Lonius), Sam Jenkins (Kirin), David Press (Garas), Nicko Vella (Marcareus), Tom Agree (Styros), Vanessa Valentine (Mountain Maiden), and Steven Wright (Scarred Man)

When Hercules is struck by one of Hera's bolts of lightning, he loses his memory and is convinced that he is actually Prince Milius. Hera's plan is to make him believe he is Milius until Equinox Day, when he will pledge his loyalty to her and in turn be her slave forever. Iolaus does his best to save Hercules from this fate but has numerous obstacles thrown in his way, most notably slipping into a vat of wine and spending most of the story line colored purple.

Behind the Scenes "This was actually a story that Rob Tapert's assistant came up with," says Robert Bielak. "The way he originally went, it wasn't quite *Hercules* and didn't serve us. We kind of went back to elements of the story, had him do rewrites, and then I subsequently rewrote it and took it in a different direction. He had really good elements in that story that we wanted, which was, again, getting our guy to fall in love with somebody. And getting to that moment when the realization is there that it wasn't going to work. Our guy just can't seem to get laid. What kind of life is this? I like the way it turned out. I thought there were some funny things with Iolaus where he went off to a wine festival and became the purple man. Just a funny episode to write, and it still gave you some heart. Not quite as much action as we usually have, but enough to get by.

"One thing the episode did do was get Kevin out of his leather pants," he adds. "Kevin got to wear a princely outfit, which he was eternally grateful for. But the whole bit of business of people bowing down to him and treating him royally, and he's feeling really strange about it; he's not really sure he's who the people are saying he is. So it gave him the chance to do some different things. That was what we were looking for at this point, just trying to get him to stretch a little bit and get out of that weekly heroic go-out-and-slay-the-monster mode and just give him some different things to play. I thought it worked well."

Episode #46: "A Star to Guide Them"

Teleplay by John Schulian and Brian Herskowitz
Story by John Schulian
Directed by Michael Levine
Guest Starring Denise O'Connell (Queen Maliphone), Edward Newborn (King Polonius), Jon Brazier (Trinculos), Kirstie O'Sullivan (Loralie), Sam Williams (Comrade), and Vickie Bennett (Old Woman)

When his oracle informs King Polonius that a newborn child will someday dethrone him, he and his wife Queen Maliphone issue a decree that all newborn children will be brought to the castle and executed. Of course Hercules and Iolaus can't stand by and let such a thing happen. At the same time, Iolaus' palms have turned red, and he is being led somewhere with two other people. After the children are set free and Polonius and Maliphone are stopped, Hercules follows Iolaus and the others, who are led by the Northern Star to a stable.

Behind the Scenes "My farewell episode," says John Schulian. "Everyone was worried that it hewed too closely to the Christmas story. I think after I was gone Bob Bielak and Brian Herskowitz made some pretty significant changes to the story. Whatever happened, I don't know. I haven't watched *Hercules* since I left the show."

Episode #47: "The Lady and the Dragon"

Written by Eric Strin and Michael Berlin
Directed by Oley Sassone
Guest Starring Catherine Bell (Cynea), Rene Naufahu (Adamis), Alexander Gandar (Gyger), Charles Pierard (Lemnos), Phaedra Hurst (Leandra), Grant Tilly (Toth), Bryce Berfield (Bartender), and Graham Smith (Marcius)

A man named Adamis has trained a dragon to attack and destroy villages. Hercules and Iolaus set out to stop him and destroy the dragon until they realize that the beast is a child that wants nothing more than to return home. The dragon is being manipulated by Adamis, who is pretending to be its friend but, in actuality, is the one who murdered the dragon's mother.

Episode #48: "Long Live the King"

Teleplay by Sonny Gordon
Story by Patricia Manney
Directed by Timothy Bond
Guest Starring Roger Oakley (King), Lisa Ann Hadley (Niobe), Derek Payne (King Xenon), Walter Brown (King Phaedron), Peter Ford (Borea), Ronald Hendricks (Choleus), and David Downs (Cleitus)

Iolaus' cousin (and double) Orestes is assassinated on the eve of signing a pact with several other leaders to create the League of Kingdoms. Iolaus, reunited with Queen Niobe, whom he had developed feelings for on their first meeting, decides to uncover the truth behind this murder and learn who is trying to destroy his cousin's dream of peace.

Episode #49: "Surprise"

Written by Alex Kurtzman
Directed by Oley Sassone
Guest Starring Hudson Leick (Callisto), Liddy Holloway (Alcmene), Jeffrey Thomas (Jason), Kevin Smith (Iphicles), and Paul Norell (Falafel)

In a bid for immortality, Callisto agrees to do what Hera has asked of her: to kill Hercules. She begins by poisoning his friends and family and then leading him to the Tree of Life, which grows a special apple that can cure the poison that afflicts them. Nothing, naturally, is as easy as it seems, as Hercules has a variety of adversities he must overcome to achieve his goal before everyone he cares about is dead.

Episode #50: "Encounter"

Written by Jerry Patrick Brown
Directed by Charlie Haskell
Guest Starring Kevin Smith (Ares), Sam Jenkins (Serena), Joel Tobeck (Strife), David Mackie (Hemnor), and Steve Hall (Nestor)

Ares' nephew, Strife, makes an "illegal" (in the sense that the other gods would disapprove) deal with Prince

Nestor to kill the Golden Hind for its blood, which has the power to cause the death of gods. Strife's deal is that if the Hind is killed, he will help Nestor kill Hercules. As things turn out, Hercules helps the Hind escape Nestor's soldiers while the Hind, taking the human form of Serena, helps Hercules and Iolaus. In the end, Nestor is killed by one of his own traps, much to Ares' amusement.

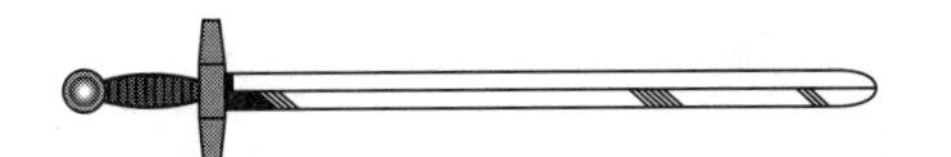

"No matter how good the show is, the script probably was better because it had more of the grace notes and humor and all the stuff that they couldn't fit in because of time constraints."
—Co-executive Producer Robert Bielak on "The Other Side"

Episode #51: "When a Man Loves a Woman"

Written by Gene O'Neill and Noreen Tobin
Directed by Charlie Haskell
Guest Starring Sam Jenkins (Serena), Joel Tobeck (Strife), Tawny Kitaen (Deianeira), Ted Raimi (Joxer), Kevin Smith (Ares), Paul McIver (Aeson), and Rose McIver (Ilea)

In the second part of this story arc, Hercules and Serena decide that they want to get married, but to do so they must strip themselves of their extraordinary powers and live the rest of their lives as mortals.

Episode #52: "Judgment Day"

Written by Robert Bielak
Directed by Gus Trikonis
Guest Starring Sam Jenkins (Serena), Lucy Lawless (Xena), Renee O'Conner (Gabrielle),

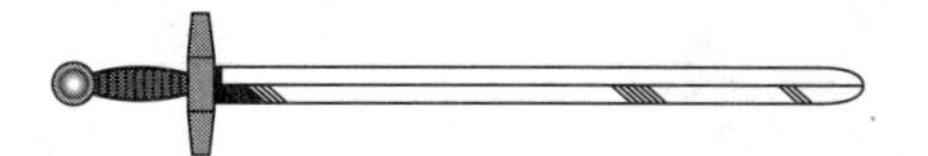

"One day I was in the shower and I saw these horses blowing smoke and fire out of their nostrils, charging through the dark, pulling this chariot. From there it all kind of fell into place."
—Co-executive Producer Robert Bielak on "Highway to Hades"

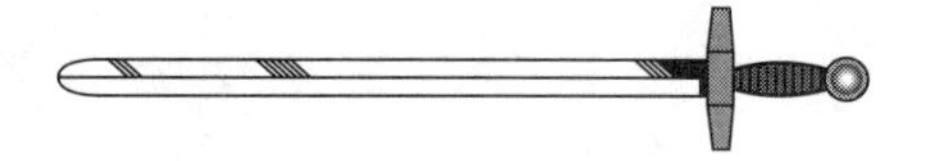

Kevin Smith (Ares), Joel Tobeck (Strife), and Peter Vere-Jones (Zeus)

In the conclusion of this story line, the now mortal Hercules gets into a fight and actually has to be rescued by Iolaus, which, surprisingly, causes him no small amount of resentment (caused, it's later revealed, by Strife). The next morning, Hercules awakens with the corpse of Serena next to him and believes that he has somehow murdered her. The villagers start to hunt him down while Iolaus, accompanied by Xena and Gabrielle, try to take him to the safety of a cave. Eventually, Hercules learns that Serena was killed by Strife, and he is plagued by guilt. At episode's end, Zeus returns his powers to him.

Behind the Scenes Notes Robert Bielak, "I think it turned out well. Poor Herc. Not only can 'Prince Hercules' not fall in love, but Herc finally does fall in love, and she's taken away from him. Worse, he thinks it's his fault. That was part of our trilogy. Rob wanted to get into this trilogy of taking his powers away for a while, then having him fall in love with this girl, and really just pushing him to the edge of despair. What is the cost of being a hero? We keep coming back to that to lend a little juice to it. Our guy is kind of like the Lone

Ranger, but the Lone Ranger and most cowboy heroes never had any angst about what they did, they just did it. Kevin can give us that angst and give us that perspective of 'Being a hero is nice on one hand, but there's a cost to it.' We like to play that, and I think it works when he plays it. These were very serious things, but I think the character of Strife added some levity to it. He was kind of a punk rock guy, a wannabe who just could never be but has these delusions that if he can't take Ares' place, he can certainly be his second in command. He could never do it, but it was funny to watch his little machinations and the stuff he got into.

"The same girl, Sam Jenkins, who played the Princess in 'Prince Hercules,' is cast in this because the chemistry between her and Kevin was so great. In real life they ultimately became an item. Sam had a little more problem because of having to play the Golden Hind in this. I don't think Sam is married to being a method actor, but I think she tends toward it. There ain't no Golden Hinds out there for her to study, and I think that kind of threw her. She didn't quite know how to grab on to that role and make it her own. I think even when she became totally human, it overflowed from the problem she had playing the Hind. That's not to say she did a bad job. When you see her, you can almost feel the uneasiness she had with playing that role. It was hard for her because she had to be in makeup for hours and hours before she could even start her day. Not an easy time for her. She did a decent job. In the end it might not have been the greatest performance in the world, but it was good. After she made the transition and left the Hind behind, then you go into the emotional beat that she's so happy, then she dies and it's a loss for Hercules. How much can one man endure? Hopefully you get a tear from the audience."

Episode #53: "The Lost City"

Teleplay by Robert Bielak
Story by Robert Bielak and Liz Friedman
Directed by Charlie Haskell
Guest Starring Robert Trebor (Salmoneus), Fiona Mogridge (Moria), Amber Sainsbury (Regina), and Marama Jackson (Aurora)

Salmoneus, Iolaus, and Moria enter a vacant temple and ultimately find themselves in caverns beneath it that are part of an underground city, the populace of which behaves like brainwashed drones. They learn that the "god" of this territory is actually a ruthless maniac known as Karkis the Butcher, who has taken control of the people there and is mining the gold that is there in abundance for his own purposes. The trio must stop him and restore mental freedom to the people "serving" Karkis.

Behind the Scenes "Kind of like the sixties comeback episode," muses Robert Bielak. "What if Timothy Leary had delusions of grandeur? It was a fun episode. It didn't quite turn out as well as I wanted it to, and I'm not really sure why. Originally this was written for Kevin, but this was at the point where he was either shooting *Kull* or at the NATPE convention. We were running into scheduling problems with him, so originally it was going to be him having his crisis of conscience or coming out of the encounter of the 'Judgment Day' episode, but he couldn't do it, so we gave it to Michael. Although Michael did a great job with it, somehow I think it lost a little of the resonance of Hercules, again looking inside himself and wondering if it is worthwhile to keep going and being a hero, and the cost of it. We had done it once before a little bit on 'Gladiator,' where he took a beating in a sense out of the guilt he was feeling, as shown in flashbacks he was having to his family being killed by Hera's fireball and the feeling of responsibility for that. He was almost paying penance, even though he could have just ripped out his bonds and tore the whip out of the guy's hands. He decided to take the punishment.

"I did think the last fight of the episode with the strobe-light effect was pretty good. That was another thing; Kevin at the time, because of *Kull,* had taken sword-fighting lessons, so this was built kind of with that in mind—let's show off his sword-fighting abilities. This whole thing was supposed to end with this great sword fight with the strobe effect. I thought it worked well with Michael, but it was originally built for Kevin."

Episode #54: "Les Contemptibles"

Written by Brian Herskowitz
Directed by Charlie Haskell
Guest Starring Robert Trebor (Francois), Danielle Cormack (Chartreuse Fox), Patrick Nelson (Captain Gerard), Phil Sorrell (Criminal), Mark Perrett (Executioner), and Robert Lee (Guy)

This episode, taking place in Troyes, France, circa 1789, is a change of pace episode in which a man claiming to be the famous Chartreuse Fox tries to convert a pair of inept robbers (portrayed by Kevin Sorbo and Michael Hurst) into fighters for right by telling them the tales of Hercules and Iolaus.

Episode #55: "Reign of Terror"

Written by John Kirk
Directed by Rodney Charters
Guest Starring Robert Trebor (Salmoneus), Rainer Grant (Penelope), Alexandra Tydings (Aphrodite), Grant Bridger (King Augeus), Bruce Phillips (Palamedes), and Les Durant (Soldier Number One)

When King Augeus loses his mind and starts believing that he is Zeus, he transforms one of Aphrodite's temples into one designed to worship Hera, which doesn't sit too well with either Hercules or Aphrodite. When Aphrodite renovates to her own liking, Hera gets ticked off and endows Augeus with the powers of a god, which he must use to kill Hercules.

Episode #56: "The End of the Beginning"

Written by Paul Robert Coyle
Directed by James Whitmore, Jr.
Guest Starring Bruce Campbell (Autolycus), Kevin Smith (Ares), and Kara Zediker (Serena)

Magic crystals send Autolycus and Hercules several years backward in time, where Hercules unexpectedly gets the opportunity to save Serena's life by forcing Ares to make her mortal. The result is that she will have no memory of Hercules. Indeed, when he returns to his own time period, he sadly sees that she has married another and has a family of her own. There is some solace, though, in the fact that she is alive.

Episode #57: "War Bride"

Written by Adam Armus and Nora Kay Foster
Directed by Kevin Sorbo
Guest Starring Lisa Chappel (Melissa), Josephine Davison (Alexa), Ross McKellar (Prince Gordius), Mark Rafferty (Acteon), Marcel Kalma (Hargus), and Chic Littlewood (Tolas)

Princess Melissa is taken to a slave ship but is rescued by Hercules and Iolaus, who take her back to her kingdom. There they are stunned to learn that Melissa's sister, Alexa, has killed their father and has been laying the countryside to waste. Hercules must take on the kingdom's army and ultimately restore order with Melissa taking royal command.

Episode #58: "A Rock and a Hard Place"

Written by Robert Orci and Alex Kurtzman
Directed by Robert Trebor
Guest Starring Lindsey Ginter (Cassus), Tony Ward (Perius), Caleb Ross (Nico), Lee-Jane Foreman (Lyna), and Sterling Cathman (Geryon)

Hercules and an accused killer, Cassus, are trapped in a cave-in. While Iolaus tries to dig them out, the gathering crowd awaits Cassus' death from his injuries or the opportunity to finish him off themselves. Hercules isn't sure the man is guilty of the crime he's accused of, a fact that Iolaus attempts to figure out himself.

Episode #59: "Atlantis"

Written by Alex Kurtzman and Robert Orci
Directed Gus Trikonis
Guest Starring Claudia Black (Cassandra), James Beaumont (King Panthius), William Davis (Skirner), Ross Harper (Demitrius), and Norman Fairley (Aurelius)

Hercules survives a doomed ocean vessel's sinking, washing up on the shores of Atlantis. There he meets Cassandra, who has been having visions of his arrival and of Atlantis' doom. Unfortunately, none of her people believe a word of what she's saying, feeling that she is a heretic. In the end, she and Hercules escape with a group of people being used as slaves, only to witness the foreseen destruction of Cassandra's home.

THE HERCLOPEDIA

An A–Z Breakdown of the Hercules Universe

Note: Unlike that of *Xena,* the continuity of *Hercules* is not as tight, and names are often reused for different characters. Sometimes a name will be used for the name of a village in one episode and for the name of a character in another (e.g., TANTALUS). Or, even more confusing, different characters in different episodes will have the same name but no relation to one another (e.g., MARCUS).

A

ACTEON: Prime Minister of Lathia. He is in on a conspiracy with Alexa of Alcinia to kill her father, King Tolas, and start a war between the two neighboring kingdoms. ["War Bride"]

ADAMIS: A warlord who had been sent into exile on the island of Tarsis. He had been defeated once before in Laurentia by Hercules. ["The Lady and the Dragon"]

AEGINA: A beautiful escaped slave girl rescued by Hercules from a temple of Hera. She was going to be executed for stealing food until Hercules came along. ["The Wrong Path"]

AELON: A soldier who is struck down in battle and then carried off by Graegus. His brother is Krytus. He later appears to his brother and his mother in spirit form. ["The Vanishing Dead"]

AESON: The seven-year-old son of Hercules. ["Hercules in the Underworld"] who was killed by Hera at the same time the queen of the gods killed the child's mother, Deianeira. ["The Wrong Path"]

AGORAPHOBIUS: The father of King Xenophobius, who was the father of King Oeneus, who was the father of King Orestes. ["King for a Day"]

ALCINIA: City where Tolas, father of Melissa and Alexa, is king. ["War Bride"]

ALCMENE: The human mother of Hercules. She had a tryst with Zeus, and the result was the half-mortal Hercules. ["The Wrong Path"]

ALEE: A boxer who works in the Golden Touch Gambling Palace. ["All That Glitters"]

ALEXA: Youngest daughter of King Tolas. With a pillow, she suffocates the sickly king, her own father, with an eye toward ruling Alcinia and declaring war with the neighboring kingdom of Lathia. [War Bride"]

ALTHEA: The sister of Deianeira. ["Hercules in the Underworld"]

AMALTHEA: Thirty-three-year-old mortal wife of the satyr Cheiron. They have three children, an infant daughter named Kora, and two boys, Peleus and Telamon. They are good friends of Hercules. ["Hercules and the Circle of Fire"]

AMPHION: A great warrior who is a friend to Hercules and Iolaus. Amphion fought a battle with them against Macedonians with King Minos. He later becomes a peace lover, speaking against violence. He marries Leah, and he performs the service at Alcmene and Jason's wedding. ["The Sword of Veracity"] ["The Wedding of Alcmene"]

AMPHITRYON: The original mortal husband of Alcmene. According to the original Greek myth, Zeus took the form of Alcmene's husband in order to seduce her. She didn't know at the time that it was Zeus. Amphitryon is the actual father of Iphicles.

ANDIUS: The servant in the bachelor hideaway of Orestes. ["King for a Day"]

ANIA: Iolaus' fiancée. She is around twenty years old and quite pretty, but she can't cook, can't sew, and isn't good with animals. Iolaus is madly in love with her anyway. ["Hercules and the Amazon Women"]

ANTEUS: He is twelve feet tall and made of raw earth and leafy plants. He uses human trophies to build shrines. He gets his strength from his mother, the Earth. Hercules fights him and defeats him by holding him above his head and not letting him touch the earth. ["Hercules and the Circle of Fire"]

ANUKET: An Egyptian princess who is in Attica searching for the stolen mummy of the pharaoh Ishtar. She is the daughter of Ramses the Third, Pharaoh of Egypt. ["Mummy Dearest"]

APHRODITE: Mother of Cupid, half-sister of Hercules. She is the goddess of love, a beautiful woman who looks twenty-something and speaks like a California valley girl. She is first seen surfing toward shore on a large conch shell. ["The Apple"]

ARACHNIPHOBIUS: The father of King Agoraphobius, who was the father of King Xenophobius, who was the father of King Oeneus, who was the father of King Orestes. ["King for a Day"]

ARCADIA: The kingdom where Xena says she wants to halt Petrakis and prevent the warlord's plans for conquest. ["The Warrior Princess"]

ARCARIOUS: The assassin brought in by King Xenon to kill King Orestes. He succeeds, but when Iolaus steps in to replace King Orestes, King Xenon thinks that the assassin failed. He's given one more chance but is later killed to cover his tie to King Xenon. ["Long Live the King"]

ARCHIAS: A general under Prince Minos who also acts as his advisor. ["King for a Day"]

ARCHIVUS: One of Jason's Argonauts. He is the archivist who writes down all their activities for posterity. He is present at Jason and Alcmene's wedding. ["The Wedding of Alcmene"] ["Once a Hero"]

ARES: Son of Zeus. God of war. His nephew, Strife, shares his predilection for violence. Ares is also the half-brother of Hercules. He is also the protector of the last Golden Hind, Serena. ["Judgment Day"] ["Ares"] ["The End of the Beginning"] ["Two Men and a Baby"] ["When a Man Loves a Woman"]

ARGEAS: A tavern owner who stands up to Goth, the barbarian chieftain, who stabs Argeas in the back with a spear. ["The Siege at Naxos"]

ARMUS: An old warrior whom Hercules and Iolaus agree to help by tilling his fields. ["The Vanishing Dead"]

ARTEMIS: Goddess of the hunt. She appears wearing animal skins and sporting a bow and arrow. She offers to make Iolaus the greatest warrior in the world if he chooses her as the winner in Aphrodite's beauty contest. ["The Apple"] At one point Aphrodite wants to be the goddess of the hunt. ["Love Takes a Holiday"]

ARTEMUS: One of the Argonauts (of Jason fame). He was in love with Glauce, but Jason left his wife, Medea, to be with Glauce first. Medea murdered Glauce out of jealousy. ["Once a Hero"]

ARTUS: A boxer in ancient Greece who is killed in the ring by Eryx. ["Hercules in the Underworld"]

ASCLEPIUS: The cousin of Hercules. ["Lost City"]

ASPHODEL MEADOWS: One of the realms of the Underworld, which is ruled by Hades. ["The Other Side"]

ATALANTA: A woman who is strong enough to pick up Hercules. She once worked as a blacksmith. She is the aunt of Damon, a young Spartan who Hercules meets on a battlefield when Herc breaks up a battle between the Spartans and the Eleans. Atalanta wants Hercules to end the war between Sparta and the Eleans. ["Ares"] ["Let the Games Begin"]

ATHENA: Goddess of wisdom. She appears in a conservative dress with her hair in a bun. But the librarian-type clothing does not cover her beauty. Artemis calls her a nerd. She offers to make Iolaus the wisest man in the world if he chooses her as the winner of Aphrodite's beauty contest. ["The Apple"]

ATLANTIS: Island of peaceful, logical people who enjoy advanced technology and who have a prejudice against and disbelief in gods and magic, believing them to be the delusions of ignorant people. The island is ruled by Panthius. The people of Atlantis dress, think, and behave alike. Their actions and beliefs are controlled by Panthius. Outsiders are not allowed on Atlantis. Just about everything on the island is powered by crystals. Atlantis is destroyed by its own crystal mines, which have weakened the foundations of the island, causing it to fall into the sea. ["Atlantis"]

ATREUS: A fifty-something elder of the village of Trachis. His village is being terrorized by a misunderstood cyclops. It is he, among others, who taunted the cyclops in childhood and made him mean. ["Eye of the Beholder"]

ATROPOS: One of the three Fates. Clothos spins the thread of life, Lachesis measures it, and Atropos cuts it. Ares tries to get Atropos to cut the thread of Hercules' life but is stopped by Zeus. ["Judgment Day"]

ATTICA: The kingdom ruled by Orestes. It was ruled by Prince Minos. ["King for a Day"] The city where Salmoneus sets up a House of Horrors to capitalize on an annual feast held there. ["Mummy Dearest"]

ATTICUS: A lean, wiry, fortyish-looking farmer. After he is robbed, Hercules finds him and helps him get his money back. But it is Lucina, his wife, he has come for. She has run away from her grief of losing their two sons and is now working at Salmoneus' brother-in-law's pleasure palace. ["Under the Broken Sky"]

ATTICUS: The uncle of Iolaus and the father of Orestes. *No relation to the Atticus in "Under the Broken Sky."* ["Long Live the King"]

AUGEUS: The king who orders the dismantling of all Aphrodite's temples in his kingdom, Elis, so he can rededicate them to Hera. ["The Reign of Terror"]

AURELIUS: An agent of Ares who lures children from the village of Fallia to do the bidding of the god of war. He dies when he's fleeing Hercules and accidentally cuts himself with his own poisoned sword. ["Ares"]

AURELIUS: An old slave who has worked in the crystal mines of Atlantis. He is another sailor whose ship was thrown off course. All outsiders who come to Atlantis are secretly made slaves. ["Atlantis"]

AURORA: One of the women living in the Lost City. She doesn't like the way she sees Kamaros take advantage of the other women there. Her sister is the child-god Lorel. ["Lost City"]

AUTOLYCUS: The King of Thieves. He steals King Menelaus' prized ruby, and when Iolaus is blamed for the theft and slated for execution, Hercules brings Autolycus back to Scyros to admit his crime. ["The End of the Beginning"] ["The King of Thieves"]

AYORA: One of Salmoneus' assistants. She is also bad-man Zandar's girlfriend. ["The Fire Down Below"]

B

BAKLAVA: As in "nuttier than Athenian baklava." ["Lost City"]

BATHSHEBA: The name of Pylendor's mule. ["The Unchained Heart"]

BELLICUS: The jailer of Maxius' prison in Apropos. He dies by running into his own sword. ["Gladiator"]

BERAEUS: New king of Zebran. His father was King Palos. His fiancée is Ramina. He threatened Ramina's village to get her to promise to marry him. He dies fighting Hercules, Tarlus, and Tarlus' men. ["Promises"]

BETHOS: Kingdom ruled by Polonius and his wife, Queen Maliphone. When Polonius is killed by his own death squad engineered by Hera to fight Hercules, law decrees that a new king be elected. Queen Maliphone is forced to step down. ["A Star to Guide Them"]

BLEDAR: The brother of Goth, the barbarian chieftain. He plans to free his brother from the imprisonment of Hercules. ["The Siege at Naxos"]

BLOOD-EYES: The name of the cult of Hera-worshipers who wear a red peacock emblem on their uniforms. They stole the Golden Fleece from Corinth. ["Once a Hero"]

BLUE PRIEST, THE: One of Hera's minions who tries to stop the wedding between Jason and Alcmene and murder Hercules. He claims he was killed by Hercules, and Hera brought him back to life to do her bidding. ["The Wedding of Alcmene"]

BLUTH: A warlord who employs Klepto. Hera tries to get Bluth to take Echidna and Typhon's baby Obie and give Obie a taste of blood so he will become a true monster. Bluth dies on his own sword. ["Monster-Child in the Promised Land"]

BORNUS: He is the witness to a crime when Trilos is robbed by Thanis, though actually it is Proteus in the form of Thanis. ["Protean Challenge"]

BORON: The flunky of King Xenon. ["Long Live the King"]

BRAXIS: The name of the orphaned dragon that is being manipulated for evil purposes. ["The Lady and the Dragon"]

BREANNA: A young woman who lives in the village of Plinth. Her father is Septus. ["Cast a Giant Shadow"]

BRONTUS: An Elean warrior who is fighting against Sparta. ["Let the Games Begin"]

BROTEAS: The leader of a group of refugees that arrives in the ghost town of Parthus. When he steals a golden chalice from the temple of Hera, it brings the wrath of Hera down on all of them. ["The Road to Calydon"]

C

CALLISTO: Victim of Xena's evil army, Callisto watched her family die and vowed revenge against Xena by becoming not only like Xena but completely consumed by hatred and lust for revenge, violence, and murder. ["Surprise"]

CALYDON: A city just beyond the Stymphalian Swamp. Hercules offers to guide a band of refugees there. ["The Road to Calydon"]

CANTHUS: A villager who drinks a toast to Hercules for destroying Eryx. ["Hercules in the Underworld"]

CASSANDRA: A young woman about twenty years old who lives away from the main city on the island of Atlantis. She has the gift of prophecy and is shunned by the logic-minded Atlantean people. She predicts the destruction of Atlantis and tries to warn them, but they won't listen. She becomes the only survivor of the fallen Atlantis. ["Atlantis"]

CASSITA: One of the kingdoms that King Orestes wanted to sign his League of Kingdoms peace treaty. ["Long Live the King"]

CASSIUS: A centaur who is forbidden by law to consort with his human lover, Myrra. He is a natural leader with a hot temper and plans on fighting for centaur rights in Myrra's village. He is not above using violence to get his rights. Ceridian was his mentor. ["Centaur Mentor Journey"]

CASTOR: Overseer of Hera's vineyard. He has employed a misunderstood cyclops to defend the vineyard and make sure the dammed-up river keeps running toward it, a river that a village called Trachis also depends on for its farms. He is killed by one of Hera's executioners. ["Eye of the Beholder"]

CASTOR: One of the Argonauts (of Jason fame). He turns traitor, kills Lycenus, Otus, and Valerus and steels the Golden Fleece. Until he is unmasked, he disguises himself as a demonic warrior. He is killed in a fight with Jason. ["Once a Hero"]

CATACOMBS, THE: The deadly maze beneath the palace of the warlord Gorgus. Hercules enters there to get to the dungeon where Iolaus has been imprisoned. Hercules has a battle there with the Mandrake. ["What's in a Name?"]

CECROPS: A king whose dying words swore vengeance against Hercules. Threats of the presence of his ghost are used to frighten people. In Attica an annual festival is held to scare away the ghost of King Cecrops. *Not to be confused with the Cecrops seen on Xena.* ["Mummy Dearest"]

CERBERUS: The three-headed dog that guards the Underworld. ["Hercules in the Underworld"]

CERIDIAN: An old centaur mentor who is about to die. He is the one who helped raise Hercules and taught him everything he knows about archery, swordsmanship, medicine, philosophy, reading, and writing. He was also a mentor to Jason, Cassius, and the young Theseus. When he dies, he is mourned by many great people. ["Centaur Mentor Journey"]

CERYNEIA: A village whose people want to destroy the last Golden Hind. ["Encounter"]

CHARIDON: An old man that Hercules and Iolaus find chained to a cell wall inside Fort Parapet. ["The Siege at Naxos"]

CHARON: The boatman who takes people across the river Styx to the Underworld. ["Hercules in the Underworld"] ["The Other Side"]

CHARTREUSE FOX: A revolutionary who leaves a yellow rose as his calling card. Francois Demarigny (Salmoneus) tells Marie Devalle that he is the Chartreuse Fox, when in reality it is Marie all along who is the "Fox." ["Les Contemptibles"]

CHEIRON: An immortal satyr who is a warrior and old friend of Hercules. His wife is Amalthea, and his children are Pelius, Telamon, and Kora. He has a never-healing wound that Hercules tries to heal with water from a magical fountain. But the wound persists. Because Cheiron is an immortal, the only way he can have a never-healing wound is if the wound is inflicted by another immortal. We find out that it was Hercules who, while fighting at Cheiron's side, inflicted the wound accidentally. Later, with a special fire that destroys immortals, Cheiron is made mortal, and his wound heals. ["Hercules and the Circle of Fire"]

CHEIRON: According to Greek myths, Cheiron the centaur educated the young Hercules while he was kept hidden from the wrath of Hera.

CHERIS: Penelope's bridesmaid and a good friend of Tyron, a young soldier who has brought home the armor of his fallen comrade to his surviving family. ["As Darkness Falls"]

CHILLA: A martial arts instructor in the Amazon village. ["Hercules and the Amazon Women."]

CHIRON: The brother of the centaur Nessus. ["Hercules in the Underworld"]

CHOLEUS: A lout who sees Iolaus, mistakes him for King Orestes, and kidnaps him with the aid of his companion Cleitus. ["Long Live the King"]

CLARION: A lean, middle-aged villager who, along with a large group of refugees, is trying to escape King Melkos' vicious reign. He is part of the rebellion against the king. ["Heedless Hearts"]

CLEITUS: A lout who sees Iolaus, mistakes him for King Orestes, and kidnaps him with the aid of his companion Choleus. ["Long Live the King"]

CLEMITUS: A courtesan to King Phaedron. ["Long Live the King"]

CLETIS: A boxer's companion in ancient Greece. ["Hercules in the Underworld"]

CLETIS: A centaur-hater. He's a vendor who won't sell to Lyla because she loves centaurs. He helps burn down Deric and Lyla's house, and the resulting fire kills Lyla. Deric kills him but claims it is an accident. ["Outcast"]

CLYTUS, FARMER: He helps set up the village for a festival with Hercules and Iolaus. He has two beautiful daughters who interest Iolaus. ["The Enforcer"]

CORINTH: The kingdom ruled by Jason (of Argonauts fame). ["Once a Hero"] Where Iphicles, the brother of Hercules, lives with his wife. ["Love Takes a Holiday"] Where Hercules and Iphicles were born. Iphicles is named King of Corinth by Jason. ["The Wedding of Alcmene"] Corinth is revisited in "Surprise."

CRAESUS: A young centaur who helps Nemis kidnap Penelope and her bridesmaid, Cheris, and exact revenge on Hercules. Hercules kills him with a well-placed arrow as the centaurs attack him, Marcus, and Salmoneus. ["As Darkness Falls"]

CRETUS: A lieutenant in the army of Xena. He is killed by Spiros. ["The Gauntlet"]

CRETUS: A traveler who lost everything gambling in Midaseus. ["All That Glitters"]

CROISANT: He looks exactly like Falafel, only he sells rodent crepes in 1789 Troyes, France. ["Les Contemptibles"]

CRONOS STONE, THE: A precious gemstone in King Quallus' collection. It has time-travel and time-freezing properties. ["The End of the Beginning"]

CYCLOPS: A one-eyed giant who terrorizes villagers in Trachis. Hercules learns he is simply misunderstood and lonely and convinces the villagers to stop teasing him if he will stop terrorizing them. He falls in love with the village seamstress, Scilla. ["Eye of the Beholder"]

CYLLABOS: The village where Leandra lives. Hephaestus put the entire village into limbo for fifty years when she turned down his proposal of marriage. ["Love Takes a Holiday"]

CYNEA: A femme fatale who lures men into fighting a dragon. Iolaus encounters her on his way to Laurentia. She is secretly working for her brother Adamis, who accidentally kills her while he's sword fighting with Iolaus. ["The Lady and the Dragon"]

CYPRUS: Aphrodite gets a letter signed "Sleepless in Cyprus." ["Love Takes a Holiday"]

CYRENEIA: Home of Serena, the Hind, where she and Hercules lived while married. Hercules and Autolycus end up in a past version of this kingdom when Autolycus uses the Cronos Stone to travel through time. ["The End of the Beginning"]

CUPID: A twentyish, unshaven, tattooed, rebellious god whose arrows cause people to fall in love. He is the son of Aphrodite. He is in love with Psyche. His jealousy of Psyche's love for Hercules causes him to turn into a green-eyed monster. ["The Green-Eyed Monster"]

D

DAEDALUS: An inventor who becomes embittered after one of his inventions accidentally causes the death of his fourteen-year-old son. He lives in the city of Euboea. Hercules finally makes Daedalus see the error of his ways. ["Doomsday"]

DAMON: A Spartan who is knocked unconscious by Brontus the Elean. This is how Hercules meets Damon. ["Let the Games Begin"]

DANIELLA: The beautiful daughter of the farmer/sculptor Thanis. The god Proteus falls in love with her and wants to possess Daniella at any cost, even if it means her father's life for rejecting Proteus. ["Protean Challenge"]

DAPHNE: Wife of Timuron. Timuron died on their wedding night. ["Highway to Hades"]

DARPHUS: A battle-scarred lieutenant in the army of Xena. He deposes her from command and drives her out through the gauntlet. Later Xena confronts and kills Darphus in battle. ["The

Gauntlet"] Killed by Xena, he is returned to life by Ares to become a brutal assassin/warrior. He's eaten by Graegus, whereupon the dog of war splits in two. ["The Unchained Heart"]

DAULIN: The twenty-five-year-old son of King Memnos. His sister is Poena. When Daulin's father dies, Ares manipulates them to think that each is responsible for King Memnos death in order to cause them to go to war against each other. ["The Vanishing Dead"]

DAX: One of Goth's barbarian guards. ["The Siege at Naxos"]

DEIANEIRA: The first wife of Hercules. She and his children were killed by a vengeful Hera, who hurled a ball of flames that consumed Deianeira right before Hercules' horrified eyes. ["The Wrong Path"]

DELIA: Karis' girlfriend. She is a beautiful woman whom Karis uses to tempt his half-god nephew, Deon, to join his gang of bandits. ["The Power"]

DELOS: An island off the coast of Syros. Its armaments are aimed directly at Syros, which has equal armaments aimed at the island. The two cities have had a history of war. ["The Apple"]

DELPHI: Where the legendary oracles are found in ancient Greece.

DEMARIGNY, FRANCOIS: He looks just like Salmoneus. He claims he is the Chartreuse Fox in a ruse to get at the money of the rich Marie Devalle. He is in league with Robert (Hercules) and Jean-Pierre (Iolaus). Later, they all join the Chartreuse Fox's revolution. ["Les Contemptibles"]

DEMETER: The goddess of the harvest and mother of Persephone. She has the power to control the weather, which she does to force Hercules to intervene and journey to the Underworld to rescue Persephone. ["The Other Side"]

DEMETRIUS: A thug hired by Echidna to kill Hercules. Echidna ends up killing him when he gets in her way. ["The Mother of All Monsters"]

DEMICLES: A young man in with the wrong crowd. He is there when bigots burn down Lyla and Deric's house, killing Lyla, but he is not an instigator, and his conscience knows they are wrong. He ends up fighting on the side of Hercules and Deric. ["Outcast"]

DEMITRIUS: A transport ship crew member. Hercules is traveling on his ship when it sinks from a weapon fired off the island of Atlantis. The surviving crew wash up on the shores of Atlantis and are taken as slaves to work in the mines. Hercules washes up on another beach on the island and is found by Cassandra. ["Atlantis"]

DEON: A handsome eighteen-year-old farm boy who is in love with Sirene. He and his girlfriend are attacked by bandits on the beach. He learns he has a power in his voice to command people to do his bidding. When his father finally admits to him that his mother is Aphrodite, he is angry and bitter. As a half-god and son of Aphrodite, this also makes Deon Herc's nephew. ["The Power"]

DERIC: Deric the centaur. His girlfriend is the human Lyla. He was raised by Nemis. Later, he and Lyla are married and have a beautiful centaur son named Kefor. ["The Wedding of Alcmene"]

DERK: Full name Derkus Petronicles. A murderer being escorted to Sparta by Hercules. When they are shipwrecked, Derk and Hercules become reluctant allies. ["Mercenary"]

DEROS: A scout sent by Xena to find Hercules. ["The Gauntlet"]

DEVALLE, MARIE: A young woman in her early thirties. She is beautiful, sexy, and rich. She is the real Chartreuse Fox and outfoxes DeMarigny, Robert, and Jean-Pierre. ["Les Contemptibles"]

DIADORUS: A tall, lean man in his fifties. He is king of Delos, an island kingdom that has a history of warring with its mainland neighbor, Syros. His son, Epius, is marrying princess Thera of Syros to help maintain peace between their cities. ["The Apple"]

DIONYSUS: According to Greek myths, he was the father of Deianeira, who was the second wife of Hercules.

DIRCE: A friend of Iolaus. She is the daughter of King Menelaus. When Iolaus is falsely imprisoned, she becomes his lawyer. He meets her again as she's being robbed. He invites her to accompany him to Alcmene and Jason's wedding. ["The Wedding of Alcmene"] ["The King of Thieves"]

DISCORD: An immortal who is helping Ares find Nemesis and her psychokinetically talented baby, Evander. She loves Ares and becomes jealous when she learns Evander is Ares' and Nemesis' child. ["Two Men and a Baby"]

DOMESTICLES: One of Jason's Argonauts. He is present at Alcmene and Jason's wedding. ["Once a Hero"] ["The Wedding of Alcmene"]

DRAGONS: Braxis and other dragons live on the island of Tarsis. The warlord Adamis was exiled there and befriended Braxis after killing the young dragon's mother. ["The Lady and the Dragon"]

DRAXUS: The fortress of General Archias. ["King for a Day"]

E

ECHIDNA: The mother of all monsters. Some of her "babies" include the hydra, the She-Demon, and the Stymphalian Bird. ["The Mother of All Monsters"]

ECHION: A villager who drinks a toast to Hercules for destroying Eryx. ["Hercules in the Underworld"]

EGREGIOUS: A facilitator (i.e., lawyer) who offers to represent Iolaus when he's shot with an arrow. ["Encounter"]

ELECTROCHAMBER: Panthius, king of Atlantis, puts Hercules in this chamber. It is lined with crystals that shoot blasts of fire, which he successfully dodges until he escapes by deflecting the fire with his gauntlet and creating a big hole in the wall. ["Atlantis"]

ELOPIUS: A man who asks Hercules to rescue his daughter, Melina, from the supposed monster in the Cave of Echoes. It is really Parenthesis who rescues her, and the monster turns out to be her tiny kitten named Zeus, whose wailing echoes in the strange caves sound like roars. ["Cave of Echoes"]

ELORA: A young woman found living in the abandoned Fort Parapet. Her father, Charison, is chained to a wall there. ["The Siege at Naxos"]

ELUSIUS: King Sisyphus' right-hand man. ["Highway to Hades"]

ELYSIA: The village where Darphus challenges Hercules to meet him in battle. ["The Unchained Heart"]

ELYSIAN FIELDS: The good part of the Underworld to be in. ["Hercules in the Underworld"] A paradisal world housing the souls of all good people and those who've been consigned to Tartarus who have earned their way up. ["Not Fade Away"] ["When a Man Loves a Woman"]

EMISSARY: An agent of Ares, the god of war, sent to return Darphus to life in exchange for agreeing to kill Hercules. He even gives Graegus, Ares' war dog, to Darphus to help him. ["The Gauntlet"]

ENFORCER: Created by Hera to take Nemesis' place and kill Hercules. She bleeds water and has a metal skeleton. ["The Enforcer"]

ENFORCER II: A strongwoman sent by Hera to kill Hercules. She is stronger, supposedly, than Enforcer I, and she kills Iolaus, prompting Hercules to go to Hades for help in not only killing Enforcer II but also bringing Iolaus back to the living world. Enforcer I is sent to fight her, but is killed by Enforcer II. Enforcer II is eventually killed by Hercules. ["Not Fade Away"]

ENOS: A nearsighted villager. ["The Unchained Heart"]

EPEIUS: A peasant who is brought before Iolaus (when he's masquerading as King Orestes) because he's behind in his taxes. The king invites Epeius and his family to stay in the palace for a time. ["King for a Day"]

EPHADON: One of a group of refugees that arrives in the ghost town of Parthus. ["The Road to Calydon"]

EPICURES: A gourmet chef who serves food that Hercules always loves. ["Highway to Hades"]

EPHINY: A peaceful Amazon who has a centaur son named Xenan. ["Prodigal Sister"]

EPIUS: Son of King Diadorus of Delos. He is marrying Thera, princess of Syros, to help bring peace between their two traditionally warring kingdoms. ["The Apple"]

EPIUS: Trachis' lieutenant in the town of Pluribus. Trachis orders him to kill Hercules and Iolaus. ["The Sword of Veracity"]

EREBUS: Someone who serves Hades in the Underworld.

EREBUS TEST: A test of innocence. It is a traditional law in Scyros, even though barbaric. Dirce gets King Menelaus to enact this law to buy Hercules time to find the real thief of the king's ruby and thus free Iolaus. The tests are near to impossible to pass, however. The first one involves dunking Iolaus into water, weighted down by a huge rock. If Iolaus drowns, he's guilty. Iolaus uses a trick he learned in the East of slowing his heartbeat to survive this test, only to discover that two more tests await him. The second test is "pressing." Iolaus must hold a door on his shoulders as guards load it with stones. He is not allowed to let any stones fall. The third test is to remain for three hours in a pit with a wild boar without spilling a drop of blood.

ERYX: A champion boxer in ancient Greece. He is seven feet tall. He kills a boxing opponent and his friends, but Eryx is then killed by Hercules. It turns out that the power of Eryx came from Hera. Hercules encounters Eryx again when he visits the Underworld. ["Hercules in the Underworld"]

ESTRAGON: One of Xena's soldiers from her early evil Xena days. When he surrenders in a fight with Hercules, Xena kills Estragon with her Chakram. ["The Warrior Princess"]

EUBOEA: The city that is the home of the inventor Daedalus. ["Doomsday"]

EURIANA: Queen of Marathon and wife of King Phaedron. She helps Iolaus escape when he's falsely accused of attempting to kill King Phaedron. ["Long Live the King"]

EURYSTHEUS: According to Greek myths, he was the cousin of Hercules and also the king of Greece. It was Eurystheus who gave Hercules the legendary twelve labors to perform.

EVANDER: One of the villagers of Trachis who is killed by the rogue cyclops. ["Eye of the Beholder"]

EVANDER: An infant in a basket who passes by Hercules in a river while Hercules is fishing. Hercules plucks him out of the water and brings him up to show Iolaus what he caught. Nemesis tells Hercules that Evander is "their" baby, but he is really Ares' son. It also seems that Evander has psychokinetic powers. He can lift objects with his mind. He also burps fire. ["Two Men and a Baby"]

EVANTHEA: A woman who Iolaus loves, but when he arrives in Parthia to visit her, she knocks him out with a bottle of wine (and the wine is still in the bottle at the time). ["Love Takes a Holiday"]

F

FALAFEL (*See also* CROISANT): A peddler whom Hercules sometimes encounters. One time he's selling sea-serpent jerky. ["The Lady and the Dragon"] The inventor of fast food. ["The Other Side"] In "War Bride," this inventive food entrepreneur is running "Falafel's Ultimate Sports Tavern and Grill." He also runs a gambling business in which his oddsmaker is named Jimius the Greek. When Hercules points out that "we are all Greek here," Falafel doesn't see the redundancy.

FELICITA: She and her baby are saved by Hercules and Iolaus, who come upon them being hassled by highwaymen. Felicita is the wife of a gladiator named Gladius. She was once Postera's slave, which is how she and Gladius met. But she was exiled, and Gladius was told she was dead. ["Gladiator"]

FIFTY DAUGHTERS OF KING THESPIUS: Hercules is being chased by King Thespius' fifty daughters because Thespius wants each one of them to have a child by him. When Salmoneus gets in their way, they settle for him, which is not too much of a problem for Salmoneus. ["Eye of the Beholder"]

FIST OF TOLAS: A horrible weapon built by King Tolas of Alcinia in his younger days while at war with Lathia. His kingdom almost did not survive it. His youngest daughter, Alexa, uses the weapon when she becomes temporary ruler to try to start another war. The Fist shoots many-pointed fleschettes from multiple magazines, all jutting from a large cart. ["War Bride"]

FLAXEN: In her twenties, she is the daughter of King Midas. She's opposed to the gambling palace that her father constructed. ["All That Glitters"]

FORT PARAPET: An abandoned Athenian fort where Hercules and Iolaus take their prisoner Goth to hold off the rescue attempt of Goth's brother, Bledar. ["The Siege at Naxos"]

G

GABRIELLE: Along with Xena, she shows up in Cyreneia just in time to find out that Hercules is accused of killing his new wife, Serena. She helps Herc and Iolaus search for the truth behind the murder. ["Judgment Day"]

GARANTUS: The kingdom ruled by King Xenon. ["Long Live the King"]

GARAS: Lonius' first lieutenant in Kastus. He helps Lonius and Queen Parnassa convince the populace that the amnesiac Hercules is really Prince Milius. ["Prince Hercules"]

GATES OF HEPHAESTUS: These gates block the last doorway from the Labyrinth of the Gods leading to the cavern housing the Tree of Life. Callisto traps Hercules between them. ["Surprise"]

GERRARD, CAPTAIN: Captain of the French police. He is hunting the Chartreuse Fox. ["Les Contemptibles"]

GLADIUS: A gladiator married to Felicita. He has a son by her who he has never seen because he was told by his slavers that Felicita died in childbirth. Instead, Felicita was exiled. She returns with Hercules and Iolaus, and the prisoners and slaves, along with Gladius, are eventually freed. ["Gladiator"]

GLAUCE: The woman Jason fell in love with and left his wife, Medea, for. But then Medea murdered Glauce. Artemus had also been in love with Glauce. ["Once a Hero"]

GLAUCUS: The surly blacksmith of the village of Trachis. He starts a fight with Hercules but is knocked flat. He hates the cyclops on general principle, and his taunts through the years have made the cyclops mean. This is why the cyclops turned against the village when Castor, the overseer of Hera's vineyard, came along. ["Eye of the Beholder"]

GNATIUS: A small-time thief who witnesses the emergence of the Enforcer. He decides he might be able to make money if he helps her find Hercules so she can kill him. ["The Enforcer"]

GNOSSUS: A member of the rebellion against King Melkos. His wife is Hephates. He is also the king's bookkeeper and Rheanna's brother. He is murdered by King Melkos' army. ["Heedless Hearts"]

GNOXIUS: The man who sold Salmoneus the "air sandal" franchise. Later, they meet again, and Gnoxius and Salmoneus go in together on a wrist sundial business they call Bolex and, later, Timodex. ["Centaur Mentor Journey"]

GOLDEN HINDS: Creatures whose blood can kill a god. They are something like a centaur. ["Encounter"]

GOLDEN TOUCH GAMBLING PALACE: The name of the gambling emporium opened by King Midas in Midaseus. ["All That Glitters"]

GORDIUS: Prince of Lathia, neighboring kingdom to Alcinia. He is to be married to the spoiled Princess Melissa to ensure peace between the kingdoms. ["War Bride"]

GORGUS: A warlord and the stepfather of Rena. He has promised Rena's hand in marriage to Pallaeus, but Rena says she loves only Hercules. Gorgus is overthrown by the combined efforts of Iphicles, Hercules, and Iolaus. ["What's in a Name?"]

GOTH: A barbarian chieftain. Hercules takes him into custody for the murder of Argeas and to Athens to stand trial. ["The Siege at Naxos"]

GRAEGUS: Ares' war dog, a huge vicious creature that likes to feast on the bodies of the dead on battlefields. He eats human flesh, and the more he eats the bigger he gets. Darphus is eaten by Graegus, whereupon the dog of war splits in two, then splits again and again until he turns to dust because the evil in Darphus canceled out the evil inside the dog of war. ["The Gauntlet"] ["Unchained Heart"] ["The Vanishing Dead"]

GREDOR: Town magistrate. He has made a law that centaurs and humans are forbidden to mix. He incites humans and centaurs to fight because if the centaurs are killed he stands to gain land. He is eventually exposed and run out of town. ["Centaur Mentor Journey"]

GREGOR: A soldier whom Hercules finds dying on a battlefield near Chaldea. Hercules agrees to the man's dying request that he take a letter to his wife, Janista, and son, Titus. ["Ares"]

GROVELUS: King Melkos' right-hand man. ["Heedless Hearts"]

GRYPHON: A village that is threatened when a hole to Hades opens in the ground. ["Hercules in the Underworld"]

GYGER: A ten-year-old boy who makes friends with Braxis the dragon. This is because the dragon is also only a youngster. Gyger is the son of Lemnos and Leandra. ["The Lady and the Dragon"]

H

HADES: God of the Underworld. ["Hercules in the Underworld"]

HARGUS: The thug who captures spoiled Princess Melissa of Alcinia and tries to sell her off to slavers. ["War Bride"]

HARPIS: A traveler who lost everything gambling in Midaseus, or at least her husband Cretus did. ["All That Glitters"]

HECATE: The sister of Hera, queen of the gods. ["The Wrong Path"]

HECTOR: A man from the Gargarensian Village who is in love with the Amazon Chilla. They have a four-year-old daughter who he has never been allowed to see. ["Hercules and the Amazon Women"]

HECTOR: The aide to Iolaus' cousin, King Orestes. He sends a message to Iolaus that says he believes that his cousin is in danger. ["King for a Day"] ["Long Live the King"]

HELIOTROPE: A woman who works in a pleasure palace. ["Under the Broken Sky"]

HEMNOR: He is from Cyreneia and comes to find Hercules to ask for help. His village wants to slay the Hind, but he wants to stop them because it is the last of its kind and harms only those who try to harm it. ["Encounter"] A friend to Hercules while he and Serena lived there as a married couple. ["The End of the Beginning"]

HEPHAESTUS: The scarred armor maker of the gods, referred to as the god of fire. He is secretly in love with Aphrodite, but the day comes when it is a secret no longer. ["Love Takes a Holiday"]

HEPHATES: A member of the rebellion against King Melkos. Her husband is Gnossus, who is killed in a skirmish. She betrays the rebellion by telling the captain of King Melkos' army, Syrus, their plans. ["Heedless Hearts"]

HERA: Queen of the gods and the wife of Zeus. She resents that Zeus had an affair with Alcmene, a mortal woman, by which a stepson, Hercules, was the result, and so has declared war on Hercules. She even slays the wife and children of Hercules using a fireball to further torment him because he opposes her evil on Earth.

HERACLES: The original Greek name of Hercules. The Romans renamed him Hercules.

HERCULES: The son of Zeus, king of the gods, and of the mortal woman Alcmene. Zeus was married to Hera when this happened, so she hates the illegitimate son of Zeus and tries to make his life miserable. When Hercules interferes with her evil plans on Earth one too many times, she slays his wife and children, causing him to vow vengeance on Hera. ["The Wrong Path"] Hercules was introduced in "Hercules and the Amazon Women."

HESAMA: One of a group of refugees that arrives in the ghost town of Parthus. ["The Road to Calydon"]

HIND, THE: A kind of half-woman, half-deer creature. All the Hinds are killed by Zeus, who fears their blood because the blood of a Hind can kill a god. One Hind survives. She is Serena, given protection by Ares, along with the ability to morph into human form. *See also* GOLDEN HINDS.

HISPIDES: A bearded lady who works at the Golden Touch Gambling Palace. She takes a shine to Salmoneus. ["All That Glitters"]

HOLIDUS: A fiftyish businessman. He is the father of Psyche. ["The Green-Eyed Monster"]

HOUSE OF HORRORS: A museum of thrills conceived by Salmoneus and set up in Attica. ["Mummy Dearest"]

HUNT OF THE DARK SUN: A ceremony in which the great stag deer of Garantus is hunted. King Xenon uses this as cover to assassinate King Orestes. ["Long Live the King"]

HYDRA: Three-headed monster that battles Iolaus in a dream in "War Bride." Earlier, Hercules and Iolaus kill the hydra in "Hercules and the Amazon Women." It appears to them first as a little girl, revealing a magical ability to shape-shift. When one of the hydra's heads is cut off, two more grow in its place. Iolaus also fights another hydra in "The Nemesis of Iolaus."

HYDRA OF LERNAEA: A monster that Hercules had to kill as part of the twelve labors of legend. He was aided by his cousin, Iolaus (a different character from the Iolaus of the TV series).

HYPPOLYTA: The Amazon Queen. She is around thirty years old. She shows Hercules, through a series of magical image-dreams, his past and how he has been taught that women are inferior to men. He challenges her to teach him another way of seeing women and tells her that through her violence and hatred she has become just the same as the men she hates. ["Hercules and the Amazon Women"]

I

IAGOS: An assistant to Hephaestus who betrays the blacksmith in order to steal the shield of Perseus. ["Love Takes a Holiday"]

ICARUS: The fourteen-year-old son of Daedalus. When the boy flew too high using the wings invented by his father, the wax on the wings melted, and the boy fell to his death. Daedalus blamed himself and became angry, bitter, and resentful, no longer caring whether the inventions he concocted were used for good or for evil. ["Doomsday"]

IDAS: A villager who drinks a toast to Hercules for destroying Eryx. ["Hercules in the Underworld"]

ILEA: A young Amazon woman who has never spoken to a man before she speaks to Hercules. She wants to know whether the stories of men and women living together are true. ["Hercules and the Amazon Women"] Ilea is also the name of Hercules' young daughter who is killed, along with her mother and brothers, by Hera. She lives now in the Elysian Fields, where Hercules sees her in the episode "When a Man Loves a Woman."

ILLEGIBUS: A doctor, King Phaedron's physician, and the cousin of Hector (the aide to King Orestes). ["Long Live the King"]

ILORAN: Hercules' cousin who lives in the Parthian province. When Hercules was just a child, Iloran's mother hid Hercules and Alcmene from Hera during one of her supernatural rages. ["The Gauntlet"]

IOLAUS: The best friend of Hercules. He is mortal but as great a warrior as Hercules, only he doesn't have super strength. First seen in "Hercules and the Amazon Women," where he dies and is resurrected.

IOLE: A young woman who comes to Hercules for help because a hole to Hades has opened near her village of Gryphon. ["Hercules in the Underworld"]

ILUS: A thirty-something man trying to get help for his village, Gargarensia, which is under siege. He is killed in the forest by a mysterious beast. ["Hercules and the Amazon Women"]

IPHICLES: The mortal half-brother of Hercules. He impersonates Hercules in Phlagra until the real Hercules puts a stop to the imposter. ["What's in a Name?"] He is the ruler of Phlagra. He shows up for Hercules' birthday party in "Surprise." He becomes Jason's successor as king of Corinth. ["The Wedding of Alcmene"]

IPICLES: A cook in a roadhouse visited by Hercules. ["The Gauntlet"]

IRONHEADS: The guards of King Midas, so named because of their metal helmets. They are actually thugs hired by the king's partners in his gambling palace. ["All That Glitters"]

ISHTAR: An Egyptian pharaoh whose mummy is stolen and taken to the city of Attica, where it is sold to Salmoneus. Ishtar is revived by Sokar (whom he kills) but is then defeated by Hercules. ["Mummy Dearest"]

ISLAND OF SILENT WOMEN: A land once visited by Archivus. ["Once a Hero"]

ISTER: A village in trouble that is being ravaged by a she-demon who turns people to stone. Lycus travels to seek the help of Hercules. When Hercules refuses, Iolaus goes in his place and gets petrified by the she-demon. ["The Wrong Path"]

IXION: A nine-year-old refugee who is traveling with a band that arrives in the ghost town of Parthus. ["The Road to Calydon"]

J

JACOBUS: A forty-year-old, handsome farmer. His brother is Karis. His son, Deon, is the result of a passionate one-night affair Jacobus had with Aphrodite. He ends up killing his bandit brother Karis to save his son's life. ["The Power"]

JAKAR: A centaur-hater. He helps burn down Lyla and Deric's house, a fire in which Lyla dies. ["Outcast"]

JANA: A beautiful young woman in a band of refugees that arrives in the ghost town of Parthus. She watches out for a young boy traveling with her named Ixion. ["The Road to Calydon"]

JANISTA: The mother of Titus and wife of Gregor. She lives in Fallia. Hercules reveals that her husband died in battle. ["Ares"]

JANUS: A young man in his twenties. He is a witch in disguise bent on killing Hercules and taking his power. ["Hercules and the Circle of Fire"]

JARTON: Joins forces with Poena to try to topple King Daulin from the throne of Tantalus. Jarton and Hercules were once friends. What Hercules doesn't realize at first is that Jarton is dead and is being impersonated by Ares, who has caused the war being fought in Tantalus. ["The Vanishing Dead"]

JASON: The hero of legend whose crew, the Argonauts, took his ship, the *Argo,* to find the Golden Fleece. Jason then became king of Corinth. Ten years later when the Golden Fleece is stolen, Jason and the Argonauts must retrieve it in order for Jason to retain the throne of Corinth. ["Once a Hero"] He is the husband of Alcmene and the friend and stepfather of Hercules and Iphicles. His adventures with the Argonauts are legendary.

JEAN-PIERRE: He looks exactly like Iolaus. Jean-Pierre, along with Robert (who looks exactly like Hercules), are highway robbers in Troyes, France, in 1789 who accidentally run into the Chartreuse Fox. Later, they join the Fox's revolution to fight the oppression of the poor. ["Les Contemptibles"]

JOHE: He runs Trader Johe's and is a friend of Ruun's uncle. ["Prodigal Sister"]

JORDIS: Husband of Rheanna. He was leader of the rebellion against King Melkos. ["Heedless Hearts"]

JOSEPHUS: A young rabble-rouser who wants the people of Phlagra to rise up against the evil warlord Gorgus. He teams up with Hercules and Iolaus and succeeds in bringing about the downfall of the warlord. ["What's in a Name?"]

JOXER: A joker of a warrior who has tried in vain to align himself with Xena. Because that hasn't worked very well for him, he decides to try Hercules. When Hercules marries Serena, leaving Iolaus alone, he tries to partner himself with Iolaus, again without success. ["When a Man Loves a Woman"]

JURIS: Friend of Iolaus who meets him at the Ptolemais festival. ["Prince Hercules"]

K

KAMAROS: The interpreter of the Teachings of Lorel for the people in the Lost City. His real name is Karkis. When Iolaus exposes him,

Karkis activates his self-destruct mechanism in the city and escapes through a secret passage. ["Lost City"]

KARA: The wife of Derk. He stops to see her when Hercules is taking him back to Sparta to be tried for murder. ["Mercenary"]

KARIS: Deon's uncle. His brother is Jacobus. Karis is a bandit intent on using Deon's power of influencing others to do his bidding. His own brother, Jacobus, kills him. ["The Power"]

KARIS, QUEEN: Wife of King Sisyphus. She has no children, and this saddens her. ["Highway to Hades"]

KARKIS: The real name of Kamaros. Also known as "The Butcher of Thessaly," a warlord who decided it was time to have a change of life, if not a change of personality. ["Lost City"]

KARROS: A friendly neighbor of Lyla's. ["Outcast"]

KATRINA: From Corinth. She is a scribe, which is a fancy name for a newspaper reporter. She acts like an annoying version of Lois Lane of *The Daily Planet,* with Hercules filling in for Superman. ["Doomsday"]

KEB: He threatens Hercules, tells him to leave Attica, then tries to use force to back up the threat. He is the protector of Princess Anuket and later dies protecting her from Sokar. ["Mummy Dearest"]

KEFOR: Young centaur son of Deric and the human Lyla. ["Outcast"]

KIRIN: Wife of the late Prince Milius, who died five years before. She is in on the ploy to make Hercules think he is Prince Milius. Later, she hates what she is doing when she realizes Hercules is really a great guy. She falls in love with him. She helps Iolaus escape the dungeon and helps Herc regain his memory. ["Prince Hercules"]

KLEPTO: A small-time thief who steals Echidna's new baby, Obie (Obstetrius). He works for the warlord Bluth. ["Monster-Child in the Promised Land"]

KLONUS: The nine-year-old son of Hercules. ["Hercules in the Underworld"] One of the children of Hercules who was killed by Hera at the same time the queen of the gods killed the child's mother, Deianeira. He lives with his mother, brother, and sister in the Elysian Fields after Hera kills the family with fireballs. ["The Wrong Path"] Hercules visits him again when he is planning to marry Serena. ["When a Man Loves a Woman"]

KRISALA: A woman who falls out of love when Aphrodite renounces her position as goddess of love. ["Love Takes a Holiday"]

KYRIAKIS: The village Iolaus walked from to get to Parthis to visit Evanthea. ["Love Takes a Holiday"]

KRYTUS: A fifteen-year-old boy who is the brother of Aelon. Krytus wants to be a scholar like his father was. But when Aelon dies in battle, Krytus wants to avenge him. ["The Vanishing Dead"]

L

LAHTI: Wife of Styros. She and her husband are attacked by bandits and saved by Hercules and Iolaus. ["Prince Hercules"]

LATHIA: A kingdom neighboring Alcinia. Lathia and Alcinia are about to go to war, and Princess Melissa of Alcinia is betrothed to Prince Gordius of Lathia to ensure peace between the kingdoms. ["War Bride"]

LAURENTIA: A village threatened by the nearby presence of a dragon. ["The Lady and the Dragon"]

LEAGUE OF KINGDOMS: A peace treaty conceived by King Orestes and Queen Niobe. It is doomed to failure because of the treachery of King Xenon. ["Long Live the King"]

LEAH: One of Trachis' servants. She claims she is a Hestial Virgin and can help Hercules and Iolaus find the correct Thalian cave, wherein resides the Sword of Veracity. She is actually Amphion's girlfriend. She had come to Pluribus to avenge the death of her parents (Trachis killed them), but Amphion taught her his peaceful ways. Later, Leah and Amphion are married. ["The Sword of Veracity"]

LEANDRA: One of the leaders of a village pillaged by bandits working under the cover of dragon attacks. Her son is Gyger. ["The Lady and the Dragon"]

LEANDRA: A woman Hephaestus once proposed to. When she turned him down, Hephaestus put a curse on her village of Cyllabos, banishing it to limbo for fifty years. She is the grandmother of Iolaus and the mother of Skouros. *No relation to the other Leandra.* ["Love Takes a Holiday"]

LEDA: One of a group of refugees that arrives in the ghost town of Parthus. ["The Road to Calydon"]

LEMNOS: One of the leaders of a village pillaged by bandits working under the cover of dragon attacks. His son is Gyger. ["The Lady and the Dragon"]

LETHAN: A twenty-five-year-old villager seeking help for his village, Gargarensia, which is under seige. He is killed while trying to escape a mysterious beast in the forest. ["Hercules and the Amazon Women"]

LEUCOSIA: A teenage girl. One of a group of refugees that arrives in the ghost town of Parthus. ["The Road to Calydon"]

LEUKOS: A war veteran who recognizes Demetrius, the man who is seducing Alcmene in order to get close to Hercules to kill him for Echidna. He is killed by one of Hera's archers sent by Echidna to kill Hercules. ["The Mother of All Monsters"]

LEURIPHONE: Lyla's sister. ["Outcast"]

LEUTIS: A young gladiator. A friend to Gladius, whom Leutis knocks out to take his place in the arena when Gladius is expected to fight to the death with a younger, stronger gladiator. Leutis defeats his opponent, Turkos, but refuses to kill him. Maxius orders them both killed, and the guards obey. Leutis dies with Turkos. ["Gladiator"]

LINUS: A lieutenant to King Orestes. ["King for a Day"] ["Long Live the King"]

LOCUS: Assistant to Perdidis. Whereas Perdidis pretends to hate centaurs because he did not want his daughter to live a life of unhappiness and prejudice by being with one, Locus pretends to be a sympathizer but is only out to regain ancestral land at the expense of centaurs, for whom he has no real concern. ["Centaur Mentor Journey"]

LONIUS: Queen Parnassas' general in Kastus. He tries to convince an amnesiac Hercules that he is really Prince Milius. ["Prince Hercules"]

LORALEI: Wife of Uris. She is in her mid-twenties and has an infant son along with older children. She and her husband try to run to save their baby from being rounded up by King Polonius, who has decreed that all infant boys be brought to the palace. ["A Star to Guide Them"]

LOREL: The god-child of the people in the Lost City. They follow the teachings of Lorel, but Lorel is really just a child, not a god, and is the sister of Aurora. Aurora wants to get Lorel out of the city and to a safer place. ["Lost City"]

LOTUS LEAF: An opiate put into the food of the people in the Lost City to brainwash them. ["Lost City"]

LUCENNE: An Amazon who is not very good at being a warrior. She dies in battle. ["Prodigal Sister"]

LUCINA: A dancer in a pleasure palace run by Salmoneus' brother-in-law. She has run away from her former life and husband, Atticus, to flee her grief in losing her two baby sons, Jason and Marcus, to a terrible fever that ravaged their valley. ["Under the Broken Sky"]

LYCASTUS: A young man who is attracted to Iole. He is jealous that Hercules is spending time with her. ["Hercules in the Underworld"]

LYCENUS: One of the Argonauts. He has a daughter named Phoebe. He dies before the ten-year reunion is held. ["Once a Hero"]

LYCIA: She is an Amazon battle leader and around twenty-eight years old. ["Hercules and the Amazon Women"]

LYCUS: Friend to Amphion. He wants to overthrow Trachis' evil reign over the town of Pluribus and free Amphion from being imprisoned for a murder he didn't commit. ["The Sword of Veracity"]

LYCUS: A farmer who traveled from the village of Ister to seek the help of Hercules. But he arrives at a bad time—right after Hera has killed Hercules' entire family. *No apparent relation to the above Lycus.* ["The Wrong Path"]

LYCUS: A friend of Hercules who was killed by Derk. But Derk said that Lycus deserved to die for the things he had done. *No apparent relation to the above Lycus.* ["Mercenary"]

LYDIA: A woman kidnapped by men dressed as satyrs. Iolaus, who's been kidnapped by the same men, meets her in their prison. ["The Nemesis of Iolaus"]

LYLA: A friend to the centaur Deric. She gives Hercules a potion that makes him blind so that Nemis can exact his revenge. Later, she marries Deric, and they have a son, Kefor. Bigots burn down their house, and she dies in the fire. She returns to her son in ghost form. Later, she comes back in full human form, saying Zeus intervened and brought her back to life. ["As Darkness Falls"] ["Outcast"]

M

MACADAMIA: Ruled by Prince Vargas until King Phaedron sacked the city and cut off the prince's head. ["Long Live the King"]

MACEOUS: A king and a neighbor of King Phaedron. He is conspiring with King Xenon to have King Orestes killed. ["Long Live the King"]

MACEUS: A scarred warrior chieftain who has a grudge against Hercules over the death of Maceus' brother, Demetrius. He kidnaps Iolaus to try to force him to reveal where Hercules is. ["Cast a Giant Shadow"]

MACHAREUS: Seven-year-old son of Prince Milius and Princess Kirin. ["Prince Hercules"]

MALIPHONE: Queen of Bethos, she is the pregnant wife of King Polonius. She is in her early thirties. She orders the roundup of all male children under the age of one after she learns that the Oracle at Delphi told her husband the heir to the throne would be an infant boy, but not her baby. ["A Star to Guide Them"]

MANDRAKE: The creature used by Hera against Hercules, but Hercules defeats it. ["What's in a Name?"]

MARCUS: Fiancé of Penelope, he helps Hercules fight the centaur Nemis. ["As Darkness Falls"]

MARCUS: The chief regent of Corinth who doesn't believe that Jason is worthy to remain as king. He conspires to topple Jason from the throne. In the end, he is pushed out a tower window and falls to his death. ["Once a Hero"]

MARCUS: A king and a neighbor of King Phaedron, he is conspiring with King Xenon to have King Orestes killed. ["Long Live the King"]

MARCUS THE MAGISTRATE: He tries Derk for murder in absentia. ["Mercenary"]

MARDUS or **MARDIS:** A three-year-old child who almost falls into a well and is saved by Hercules, who has time-traveled by way of the Cronos Stone into the past of the village of Cyreneia. He changes the past because in the original time line the child died. ["The End of the Beginning"]

MARJUS: A woman Hercules and Iolaus meet in the mud baths. She says she is from Century 1 Realty and offers them a deal on a time-share. ["War Bride"]

MARTUMUS: He was in love with Myrea, but their families kept them apart. In death, the lovers became a constellation. ["Hercules in the Underworld"]

MAXIUS: Menas Maxius is one of the wealthiest landowners in Apropos. His wife is Postera. He is a slaver who forces his slaves to fight in gladiatorial combat. He is overcome in a revolt by the gladiators and slaves, led by Hercules and Iolaus, and forced to outlaw slavery. ["Gladiator"]

MAYEM: A red-haired Amazon warrior who killed the parents of Siri and Ruun and kidnapped the former after blinding the latter. Thirteen years later, what she did is revealed, and Hercules fights her to the death. ["Prodigal Sister"]

MEDEA: Jason's former wife. He left her for Glauce, and in a jealous rage Medea killed Glauce. ["Once a Hero"]

MEGALITH: A powerful weapon invented by Daedalus. It consists of a man (Perdix) wearing stone and metal armor and a device that shoots flames. ["Doomsday"]

MEGARA: In the original Greek myths, she was the actual wife of Hercules. Hera drove Hercules temporarily mad so that he unknowingly killed his wife and children (which is considerably different from the TV version of what happened).

MEGARA: A young Amazon woman who reveals to Hercules that she is the mother of Franco, a boy sent away from the Amazon village when he was a baby to live with the men. Franco is also the son of Pithus. ["Hercules and the Amazon Women"]

MELANIPPE: The twenty-five-year-old daughter of Palamedes. She heals Salmoneus' bee sting on his rump. ["The Reign of Terror"]

MELINA: The twenty-year-old daughter of Elopius. She is lost in the Cave of Echoes, where Hercules, Iolaus, and Parenthesis come to look for her. When they find her, she's clinging to the edge of a pit in the cave, her foot caught in a root tangle. She thinks a monster has hold of her foot. ["Cave of Echoes"]

MELISSA: The eldest daughter of King Tolas of Alcinia. She is in her early twenties, pretty, spoiled, and about to be married off to Prince Gordius of the neighboring kingdom of Lathia to ensure peace between Lathia and Alcinia. Her sister, Alexa, engineers her kidnapping and subsequent sale to slavers before Hercules and Iolaus find her. She later takes her rightful place as Queen of Alcinia and marries Gordius. ["War Bride"]

MELKOS, KING: An evil ruler who taxes his people to the limit. He has made a law that they cannot leave his kingdom, along with another law that allows him the wedding night privileges of every new bride in the kingdom. A third law he has is to take every infant male and raise them to become soldiers in his army. ["Heedless Hearts"]

MEMNOS: The king of Tantalus. Hercules onced helped him defend Tantalus against an attack by Macedonians. After King Memnos dies, trouble begins in the village, including the bodies of dead soldiers missing after battles. ["The Vanishing Dead"]

MENANDER: A warrior who had fought with Hercules against Adamis. He is tricked into fighting against a dragon and is killed. ["The Lady and the Dragon"]

MENDELUK: A village once whipped into turmoil by Hera because she was displeased by the size of her temple there. ["Protean Challenge"]

MENELAUS, KING: The king of Scyros and an inventor. He imprisons Iolaus for stealing his most prized gem, a dragon's-eye ruby, but it's really Autolycus who stole it. ["The King of Thieves"]

MENISKOS: The captain of a band of soldiers who, working for Ares, are hunting for Nemesis and her psychokinetically talented baby, Evander. ["Two Men and a Baby"]

MERKUS: A centaur-hater. He helps burn down Deric and Lyla's home. It is he who kills Lyla by blocking her exits out of the burning house. Deric kills him in self-defense. ["Outcast"]

MICA: A woman who works in a pleasure palace. ["Under the Broken Sky"]

MIDAS: The king of Midaseus. His daughter is named Flaxen. ["All That Glitters"]

MIDASEUS: Ruled by King Midas and his daughter Flaxen. Midas builds a gambling palace there but finally comes to realize that this was a mistake when criminal elements move in to take control. ["All That Glitters"]

MIRIM: A woman who has been tending the injured Jordis, who had been thought dead by his wife, Rheanna, until Mirim leads her and Hercules to her farmhouse. ["Heedless Hearts"]

MOLORCHOS: A peasant boy who is caught in a trap and mortally wounded until he is revived by the power of the Golden Hind, which can heal injuries. ["Encounter"]

MORIA: A self-styled reporter who works for the *Star-Globus.* ["Lost City"]

MUMMY: A corpse treated and wrapped with strips of cloth, practiced most notably in ancient Egypt. Two thieves break into an Egyptian crypt and steal the mummy that is there. One of them later sells the mummy to Salmoneus in Attica. ["Mummy Dearest"]

MYKONOS: A friend of Iolaus. When Iolaus arrives in Parthia, he finds everyone acting strangely, and Mykonos tries to explain that the women have all rejected the men. They don't realize that this is because Aphrodite has resigned as goddess of love and therefore there is no love in the world, although Aprodite is controlling even this so that only women are affected. ["Love Takes a Holiday"]

MYKONOS: A province in Greece where slavery is illegal. It is illegal to even transport slaves through there. ["Prodigal Sister"]

MYLES: A young villager of Trachis who is trying to overcome the rogue cyclops that is terrorizing them. ["Eye of the Beholder"]

MYREA: She was in love with Martumus, but their families kept them apart. In death, the lovers became a constellation. ["Hercules in the Underworld"]

MYRRA: A young, twenty-something schoolteacher. She is in love with the centaur Cassius, but law forbids them to be together. ["Centaur Mentor Journey"]

N

NATROS: He is Tarlus' lieutenant. ["Promises"]

NAXOS: An island where Hercules and Iolaus go to fish. It was once raided by Goth and his band of brigands. ["The Siege at Naxos"]

NEIMUS: A king and a neighbor of King Phaedron. He is conspiring with King Xenon to have King Orestes killed. ["Long Live the King"]

NEMESIS: The beautiful hit woman of the gods. Her aim with a bow and arrow is impeccable. She and Hercules used to be a couple (she is Hercules' first love), and they still have affection for each other. Hercules is the one who convinces her to use a little justice in her methods of killing mortals for retribution of their acts on Earth. ["The Enforcer"] ["The Fire Down Below"] ["The Nemesis of Iolaus"] ["Two Men and a Baby"]

NEMIS: A centaur that prays to Hera to let him have Penelope, a young woman who is already marrying a human. He also wants to kill Hercules for killing his twin, a centaur who tried to rape Herc's wife. ["As Darkness Falls"]

NESSUS: A centaur who has worked for Hercules for ten years and secretly hates him. When he tries to rape Deianeira, Hercules kills him with an arrow. ["Hercules in the Underworld"]

NESTOR: Prince Nestor has been petitioned to help the people of Ceryneai kill the deadly Golden Hind. Nestor hates Hercules and blames him for the death of his brother. This is why he wants the Golden Hind: to get its blood to use against Hercules. ["Encounter"]

NIKOLOS: The despot king of Euboea. When Daedalus becomes hard-hearted after the death of his son, Icarus, King Nikolos takes advantage of this to have Daedalus invent weapons of mass destruction for him. When Daedalus invents the Megalith, King Nikolos chooses to operate it personally when he decides to kill Hercules. ["Doomsday"]

NIOBE: The wife of King Orestes. She and Iolaus fell in love the last time he showed up to help his look-alike cousin. ["Long Live the King"]

NURIAN MAIDEN: A virgin who can lure a man on a suicide mission. ["Hercules in the Underworld"]

O

OBSTETRIUS: Little multitentacled baby of Echidna and Typhon who is kidnapped by Klepto. His nickname is Obie. As long as he never gets a taste for blood, he will stay a nice little monster. ["Monster-Child in the Promised Land"]

ODEON: One of a group of refugees that arrives in the ghost town of Parthus. ["The Road to Calydon"]

OENEUS: The former king of Attica and father of Orestes. ["King for a Day"]

OLYMPICS: Annual games of skill, strength, and endurance that, we are led to believe, were invented by Hercules and named by Salmoneus. ["Let the Games Begin"]

OPION: A boxer's companion in ancient Greece. He is killed by Eryx. ["Hercules in the Underworld"]

ORACLE AT DELPHI: King Polonius travels to Delphi, where the Oracle tells him the heir to his throne will be a baby, but not a baby of his blood. This prompts Polonius and his pregnant Queen, Maliphone, to round up all the infant boys in the kingdom. ["A Star to Guide Them"]

ORENTH: A lieutenant of the warlord Adamis. ["The Lady and the Dragon"]

ORESTES: A king who is the cousin of Iolaus. His wife is Queen Niobe. He is assassinated at the orders of King Xenon of Garantus. ["King for a Day"] ["Long Live the King"]

ORESTES: A teenage boy who is bewitched by the she-demon and turned to stone before he can be helped by Iolaus. *No relation to King Orestes.* ["The Wrong Path"]

ORLON: One of the kingdoms that King Orestes wanted to sign his League of Kingdoms peace treaty. ["Long Live the King"]

OTUS: One of the Argonauts (of Jason fame). When they embark on their voyage to reclaim the stolen fleece, Otus is found dead under mysterious circumstances. ["Once a Hero"]

P

PALAMEDES: Someone whom the old man Charidon used to know. ["The Siege at Naxos"]

PALAMEDES: A forty-five-year-old, robust farmer. He is friends with the poor, mad King Augeus and tries to help him in his madness. Palamedes is also a healer. But when Hera gives King Augeus true powers, he kills Palamedes. Aphrodite puts a gold aura around him to keep his spirit from going to the Other Side. He is revived by a lightning bolt. ["The Reign of Terror"]

PALLAEUS: A young soldier who is in love with Rena, but she won't marry him because she loves Hercules. Pallaeus goes to the temple of Hera to get something that he can use against Hercules. ["What's in a Name?"]

PANTHIUS: Ruler of Atlantis. He rules with an iron fist and controls every move of every citizen of the city. Nothing is done without his approval. ["Atlantis"]

PARENTHESIS: A twenty-five-year-old, scrawny writer whom Hercules and Iolaus save from hanging. He follows Hercules and Iolaus in hopes of writing about their adventures, but mostly he just gets in the way as they recount various past events to him while traveling through the Cave of Echoes looking for Melina and the other inhabitant of the cave: a supposed monster who turns out to be a tiny kitten. ["Cave of Echoes"]

PARNASSA: Middle-aged queen of Kastus who calls on Hera to help her restore power and prestige to her kingdom, which has diminished since the death of her son, Milius, five years before. An amnesiac Hercules is convinced he is the prince, and no one questions this because the prince's death was kept a secret all this time. ["Prince Hercules"]

PARTHENON: An ancient structure in Greece. ["Let the Games Begin"]

PARTHIA: A village visited by Iolaus wherein he first sees the effects of the lack of love in the world after Aphrodite resigns as the goddess of love. ["Love Takes a Holiday"]

PARTHIS: The village where Hercules' cousin Iloran lives. ["The Gauntlet"]

PARTHUS: A ghost town cursed by Hera. When Broteas steals a chalice from Hera's temple, he brings her rage down on his band of refugees. ["The Road to Calydon"]

PATRONIUS: Chief regent of Corinth under King Jason. He wants to succeed Jason as king when he finds out Jason is marrying a commoner and by law won't be able to be king anymore. If he can keep Jason from marrying in three days, Jason also won't be able to name a successor, and Patronius will automatically become king. ["The Wedding of Alcmene"]

PAUNIUS RIVER: A river crossed by Hercules on his way to the village of Gryphon. ["Hercules in the Underworld"]

PAWNICLES: He runs the pawnshop in Midaseus, and he's doing a lot of business because people are selling everything they can to get money to gamble with. ["All That Glitters"]

PELEUS: Young son of the satyr Cheiron and the human Amalthea. His brother is Telamon, and his sister is Kora. ["Hercules and the Circle of Fire"]

PENELOPE: A twenty-year-old, beautiful woman who is about to marry Marcus. The centaur Nemis is in love with her and takes her away from her wedding by force. ["As Darkness Falls"]

PERDIDUS: Father of Myrra. He does not like the fact that his daughter was consorting with a centaur, and he threatens to kill any centaur that crosses his property to get to town. Yet he knows his daughter is right when she speaks of centaur rights, and he has some sympathy for them. He ends up marching on the side of Cassius and other centaurs to the town fountain, where it is forbidden for centaurs to drink. ["Centaur Mentor Journey"]

PERDIX: The assistant of Daedalus. Perdix is also a spy for King Nikolos to ensure that the scientist remains true to his word. ["Doomsday"]

PERFIDIA: Hera's pet sea monster. It tries to kill Hercules by eating him. This is the second sea monster Hercules has seen the insides of. This time he is joined by Jason, who is also swallowed. Perfidia is killed from the inside by the two heroes. ["The Wedding of Alcmene"]

PERSEPHONE: A nineteen-year-old woman who is kidnapped by Hades and taken to the Underworld to be his lover. Hercules goes to rescue her but learns that she doesn't really want to be rescued. She really is in love with Hades. She and Hades make a deal with Demeter that allows Persephone to live in Hades six months of the year and back with her mother six months of the year. ["The Other Side"] ["Not Fade Away"]

PERSEUS: A Greek hero. According to Greek legends, Alcmene was descended from him.

PERSEUS: Hephaestus makes a shield for him. ["Love Takes a Holiday"]

PETRAKIS: A warlord whom Xena tells Iolaus she is planning to fight with her army. Actually, Petrakis is a farmer and an old man.

Xena just used his name to apply to an imaginary warlord to stir up her army and win the sympathy of others. His son rode with Xena and died fighting in her army. ["The Warrior Princess"]

PHAEDRA: A young girl whom Hercules saves from an animal trap. She sends Hercules, who is in search of the Eternal Torch, into the path of Anteus the Giant and another dangerous path where Herc and Deianeira almost die. Hercules thinks she is Hera trying to foil his plans, but she turns out to be Zeus in disguise. ["Hercules and the Circle of Fire"]

PHAEDRON: The king of Marathon and one of the people whom King Orestes wanted to sign his League of Kingdoms peace treaty. He doesn't ordinarily allow visitors to speak to him directly. ["Long Live the King"]

PHILOMENE PIG: One of the pigs owned by Triptolemus. ["The Other Side"]

PHINEUS: A friend of Hercules whom he meets in Attica during the time of the annual festival. ["Mummy Dearest"]

PHLAGRA: A town under the domain of the warlord Gorgus. ["What's in a Name?"]

PHLEBITIS: A nickname Atalanta calls Salmoneus. ["Let the Games Begin"]

PHOEBE: One of Jason's Argonauts. She is present for Jason and Alcmene's wedding. ["The Wedding of Alcmene"]

PHOEBE: The daughter of Lycenus, the lookout for the Argonauts. She doesn't believe that her father's death was an accident. ["Once a Hero"]

PILOT: A handsome thirty-five-year-old. He is chief of the local bandits. He does not like Hercules in his town and spends a lot of time sending henchmen to kill him. Later he dies in a brawl. ["Under the Broken Sky"]

PITHUS: A villager in his fifties. He's trying to escape the mysterious terrors surrounding his village, Gargarensia, and get help. ["Hercules and the Amazon Women"]

PLATO: He appears in Iolaus' vision where Iolaus has become the wisest man in the world. ["The Apple"]

PLINTH: A village visited by Hercules and Typhon, a giant who tries to be helpful but keeps causing damage because he's so clumsy. ["Cast a Giant Shadow"]

POENA: The sister of Daulin, the king of Tantalus. She fights to topple her brother, Daulin, from the throne. ["The Vanishing Dead"]

POLONIUS, KING: The king of Bethos, the husband of Queen Maliphone. He is told by the Oracle at Delphi that the heir to his throne will be an infant boy, but not of his blood. This inspires him and his wife to round up all the male infants in the kingdom of Bethos, ostensibly to kill them. ["A Star to Guide Them"]

POSTERA: Wife of Menas Maxius. She has a thirst for blood and young, virile men who fight animals and each other in Maxius' arena. She is easily bored and always looking for more violent excitement. ["Gladiator"]

PRIMORDS: Hairy, half-man, half-beast creatures. ["Promises"]

PRINCE MINOS: He wants to be the ruler of Attica, but he'll lose this opportunity when Prince Orestes is crowned king and marries Princess Niobe. His henchman, General Archias, tries to prevent the coronation, but when that fails he goes further than Prince Minos wants him to, and Minos turns to Iolaus for help. ["King for a Day"]

PRITHEANS: People from the Pritian Valley, which was raided by renegade Amazons. ["Prodigal Sister"]

PROMACHUS: The general of King Augeus. On the order of King Augeus, he orders the dismantling of all Aphrodite's temples so they can be rededicated to Hera. ["The Reign of Terror"]

PROMETHEUS: The god of fire. He lives in a cave over a cliff. He took fire from the heavens and gave it to mankind. He guards the Eternal Torch. ["Hercules and the Circle of Fire"]

PROPONTUS: A village where Damon is taken by Hercules to get medical attention. ["Let the Games Begin"]

PROTEUS: A god who falls in love with a mortal named Daniella. He can assume any living form and only rarely adopts his true form. ["Protean Challenge"]

PROTOS: The five-year-old son of dead Prince Milius and Princess Kirin. He was still in his mother's womb when his real father died. ["Prince Hercules"]

PSORIASIS: The name that Salmoneus is using as his alias while living in Propontus. Atalanta has another name for him: "The Toad." He's hiding out in Propontus after fleeing the locals on the Argean Peninsula who questioned the honesty of the game of chance that Salmoneus was practicing there. ["Let the Games Begin"]

PSYCHE: The stunningly beautiful daughter of Holidus. Nearly all the men of the village of Malidon are trying to court her, so she remains hidden to avoid the crowds. She falls in love with Hercules, whom she has known since she was a child, but it is Cupid who has his eye on her. He is jealous of her love for Hercules, a love that Herc returns because Cupid accidentally shot him with his arrow. ["The Green-Eyed Monster"]

PURCES: Salmoneus' partner in unearthing treasures found in a cave. He is a thief. Nemesis manipulates him to walk under the swinging ax of one of his co-workers, and he dies. ["The Fire Down Below"]

PYLENDOR: A hunter and trapper. Darphus sends Pylendor to tell Hercules that Darphus is back from the dead and eager to kill again. ["The Unchained Heart"]

PYLON: The henchman of General Archias. ["King for a Day"]

PYLON: The lieutenant of the warrior chieftain Maceus. *No relation to the above Pylon.* ["Cast a Giant Shadow"]

PYRO: A monster made of fire sent to destroy Hercules. He claims that he is the one Hera sent to destroy Herc's family. Hercules kills him with a well-aimed burning pillar right between the eyes. ["The Fire Down Below"]

Q

QUALLUS, KING: This dead king of Cyreniea left behind a priceless collection of gems and other items, including the Cronos Stone, a time-travel, time-distorting device that is stolen by Autolycus. ["The End of the Beginning"]

QUINTUS: One of the warriors working with Darphus, who feeds him to Graegus. ["The Unchained Heart"]

R

RAK: Lieutenant to Rankor, the chief of a group of bandits who dress like satyrs. ["The Nemesis of Iolaus"]

RAMINA: A beautiful dark-haired woman who is King Beraeus' fiancée. She is kidnapped by Tarlus, who is the man she truly loves. ["Promises"]

RANKOR: Bandit chief of men who dress as satyrs. He is attacked by a hydra when Iolaus tricks him into going into the hydra's cave. He finally appears to be killed when Iolaus shoots an arrow into a rope and drops a basket on his head. ["The Nemesis of Iolaus"]

RANKUS: A jailer in Menas Maxius' prison in Apropos. He is killed by Gladius. ["Gladiator"]

RED PEACOCK EMBLEM: The emblem worn by the men who steal the Golden Fleece from Corinth. ["Once a Hero"]

RE-EDUCATION ROOM: Where the people get their final brainwashing in the Lost City. ["Lost City"]

REGINA: The cousin of Iolaus who runs away from home. Iolaus goes looking for her and finds her in a strange city where everyone has been brainwashed. ["Lost City"]

REMO: Brother to Uris. While Uris follows his compulsion to travel north with Iolaus, Hercules, and Trinculos, Remo takes in Uris' wife, Loralei, and her children, including the infant son whom Polonius is looking for after he decreed all male infants under one year of age be brought to his palace. Later, palace guards invade Remo's home and kidnap Loralei and her baby. ["A Star to Guide Them"]

RENA: She is in love with Hercules and refuses to marry Pallaeus because of that. But what she doesn't realize is that the man she believes to be Hercules is an imposter. Finally, Iphicles reveals the truth, and the two live happily ever after. ["What's in a Name?"]

RHEANNA: A young, beautiful woman in her late twenties. She wants Hercules to help her overthrow King Melkos, who is a vicious ruler. ["Heedless Hearts"]

RIPIS: A sometime thief with a 6-foot-9, 300-pound sidekick named Mong. ["Centaur Mentor Journey"]

ROBERT: He looks exactly like Hercules. Robert and his partner, Jean-Pierre, are highway robbers in 1789 Troyes, France, who accidentally run into the Chartreuse Fox. Later, they join the Fox's revolution to fight the oppression of the poor. ["Les Contemptibles"]

RODNIUS DANGECLES: A comedian performing at the Golden Touch Gambling Palace. ["All That Glitters"]

ROMANUS: An eight-year-old boy who is stealing apples because he's hungry but is caught by guards, called Ironheads, who plan to execute the little thief until Hercules intervenes. ["All That Glitters"]

RUUN: A young man from Sarna whose parents were murdered by renegade Amazons and his sister kidnapped to be raised by the Amazon tribe. The boy was blinded by the Amazons at the time his parents were killed, and he grew to adulthood with hatred toward all Amazons. ["Prodigal Sister"]

S

SALMONEUS: A traveling salesman of sorts who, although good of heart, manages to get himself into one scheme after another, some better advised than others. ["The Gauntlet"]

SARDON: Someone whom the old man Charidon used to know. ["The Siege at Naxos"]

SARNA: A village that was attacked by renegade Amazons and the villagers massacred. One of the survivors was a young boy named Ruun. Thirteen years later, the Amazons return, but Hercules helps to defeat them this time. ["Prodigal Sister"]

SCILLA: Seamstress of the village of Trachis. ["Eye of the Beholder"]

SEGALLUS: One of King Midas' partners in the Golden Touch Gambling Palace. He soon uses his muscle to take over and forces Midas to do his bidding, much against the king's will. ["All That Glitters"]

SEPSUS: A centaur-hater. He helps burn down Deric and Lyla's house. Lyla dies in the fire. ["Outcast"]

SEPTUS: An old man who lives in the village of Plinth with his daughter Breanna. ["Cast a Giant Shadow"]

SERA: A young woman who offers her estate as the wedding venue for Jason and Alcmene. They do not know, however, that she is in league with Hera's Blue Priest to murder Hercules. ["The Wedding of Alcmene"]

SERENA: The last Golden Hind. She is Serena in human form. Her ability to become human was bestowed upon her by Ares as protection from Zeus, who has killed all the other Hinds. Her blood can kill a god. She changes back into a Hind only if she is touched by a human or at her own will. Ares bestows permanent humanity upon her, and she eventually becomes Hercules' wife. Herc later kills her in a rage-spell inflicted upon him by Strife. ["Encounter"] ["Judgment Day"]

SESTUS: A boxing manager in ancient Greece. He is killed by Eryx. ["Hercules in the Underworld"]

SEVERUS: A shopkeeper who sells Salmoneus a copper shield in exchange for a gold bowl and a love potion. Later, he is seen chasing Salmoneus. He wants revenge because he gave the love potion to his wife, and now his wife is chasing every man in the kingdom of Elis. ["The Reign of Terror"]

SHE-DEMON: She is ravaging the village of Ister, turning people to stone and delivering their souls to Hecate in the Underworld. Hercules tracks her to her lair and battles her, turning her own power against her and causing the she-demon to be turned to stone. ["The Wrong Path"]

SHELLUS: A Hind hunter. His brother is injured, and Serena heals him, for the first time learning of her healing powers in the past time line of the village of Cyreneia. ["The End of the Beginning"]

SIDON, KING: A short, stout man in his fifties. He is king of Syros. His daughter, Thera, is marrying Epius, prince of Delos, to bring peace between their two kingdoms. ["The Apple"]

SILAUS: A worker dismantling Aphrodite's temple. ["The Reign of Terror"]

SIRENE: A pretty seventeen-year-old village girl in love with Deon. She and her boyfriend are attacked by bandits on the beach. ["The Power"]

SIRI: The sister of Ruun. She was kidnapped as a child and raised to be an Amazon warrior. ["Prodigal Sister"]

SISYPHUS: King of Corinth who tricks a young man named Timuron to take his place in Hades. He has his eye on young Timuron's widow as well. He is destined to push a boulder up a hill forever in Tartarus. ["Highway to Hades"]

SKIRNER: The head guard of King Panthius of Atlantis. He perishes along with all the other citizens of Atlantis when Atlantis sinks into the sea. ["Atlantis"]

SKOUROS: The father of Iolaus. He was killed in war. He was from the village of Cyllabos. Fifty years before Iolaus met Leandra, her village was put into limbo, but because Skouros was a toddler who'd wandered away from the village before the curse hit it, he was found alone and presumed to be abandoned. Iolaus is the one to discover that Leandra is his grandmother. ["Love Takes a Holiday"]

SOCRATES: He appears in Iolaus' vision of Iolaus as the wisest man in the world. ["The Apple"]

SOKAR: He is searching for the mummy of the pharaoh Ishtar because of the power that can be unleashed from the mummy by one who knows how to use the magic symbol it wears. But the mummy kills Sokar and steals his soul. ["Mummy Dearest"]

SORDIS: The leader of the pirate band stalking Hercules on an island. He believes that Herc knows where the treasure is that was being transported on the prison ship. ["Mercenary"]

SPAGOS: A cook in the prison of Maxius in Apropos. He is also the world's first sports announcer. ["Gladiator"]

SPARTA: A province in Greece. It goes to war with the Eleans. ["Let the Games Begin"] Where Derk is wanted for murder. When Hercules escorts Derk back to Sparta, he finds that a trial has already been held without Derk able to make a defense for himself. As a result, Hercules saves Derk from execution. ["Mercenary"]

SPHINX: A stone Sphinx blocks the entrance to the Labyrinth of the Gods. Hercules and Callisto must answer its riddle before they can pass. Fire shoots from its mouth. ["Surprise"]

SPIRO: An innkeeper who is grateful when Hercules and Iolaus get rid of the ruffians in his inn. ["The Wedding of Alcmene"]

SPIROS: He believes that Hercules is responsible for the destruction of his village and tries to kill him. When Spiros learns the truth, he goes after Darphus. In the fight, he kills Cretus. ["The Gauntlet"]

STICHIUS: A worker dismantling Aphrodite's temple. ["The Reign of Terror"]

STRIFE: The nephew of Ares and brother of Discord who is more than willing to do Ares' dirty work, up to and including killing Serena. ["Judgment Day"]

STYMPHALIAN SWAMP: A huge place that Hercules guides a band of refugees through on their way to the city of Calydon. Hercules fights the Stymphalian Bird there. ["The Road to Calydon"]

STYROS: An elderly man. He and his wife, Lahti, are attacked by bandits. Hercules and Iolaus come upon the scene and save them. ["Prince Hercules"]

STYX, RIVER: The river that Charon crosses to take the dead to Hades. ["Highway to Hades"]

SWORD OF VERACITY: A magic sword. Exposure to its blade renders one incapable of lying. It can be found in the Thalian caves. ["The Sword of Veracity"]

SYREENA: An old girlfriend of Iolaus. She marries Tremulus, much to the chagrin of Iolaus. ["The Warrior Princess"]

SYREETA: An assistant to Salmoneus. He thinks she likes him only for his money, but when he loses all his money, she still says she would like to be with him. ["The Fire Down Below"]

SYROS: A city on the mainland that sports a fortified castle with armaments aimed at the nearby island of Delos. These two cities have a history of war with each other. ["The Apple"]

SYRUS: Captain of King Melkos' military. ["Heedless Hearts"]

T

TANTALUS: A village where a battle has been fought, but the bodies of some of the dead soldiers have disappeared. This is because they are being stolen by Graegus, Ares dog of war. Ares is the one who has caused the war being fought there. ["The Vanishing Dead"]

TANTALUS: A prisoner in the Underworld who is helped by Hercules, who gives him food and water to relieve the man's torment. ["The Other Side"]

TAPHIUS: An old friend of Hercules whom he met at the Battle of Dardania. He doesn't think that the Olympics is a good idea because the Eleans are tools of Ares who live only to fight and kill, egged on by their leader, Tarkon. ["Let the Games Begin"]

TARKON: The general of the Elean army. He is a ruthless agent of Ares who lives only to fight and kill. ["Let the Games Begin"]

TARLUS: Tarlus is a warrior who has kidnapped Ramina and is holding her for a ransom of ten thousand dinars. He is an old friend of

Iolaus and Hercules, but ever since he abandoned Iolaus in a battle, Iolaus has been angry with him. They meet again when Iolaus and Hercules confront him to get Ramina back. It turns out that Ramina is in love with Tarlus and that the kidnapping is a willing abduction. When Tarlus explains that he left Iolaus to protect the king but that the king was humiliated and made Tarlus promise never to tell anyone, he forgives Tarlus. ["Promises"]

TARSIS: An island where the warlord Adamis was sent into exile. It is an island populated by dragons. ["The Lady and the Dragon"]

TARTARUS: The land of fallen heroes. The bad part of the Underworld. ["Hercules in the Underworld"]

TELAMON: The young son of the satyr Cheiron and the human Amalthea. His brother is Peleus, and his sister is Kora. ["Hercules and the Circle of Fire"]

TELES: One of a group of refugees that arrives in the ghost town of Parthus. When Ixion gets lost, he offers to help Jana find him. ["The Road to Calydon"]

TEMECULIS: A city that Hercules goes to for a feast being held there. Iolaus cannot come along because he's been summoned to help his cousin King Orestes. ["Long Live the King"]

TERSIUS: A town magistrate who wants Deric the centaur brought in for murder. ["Outcast"]

THADDEUS: A security guard at the Golden Touch Gambling Palace. ["All That Glitters"]

THADEUS: Someone whom the old man Charidon used to know. ["The Siege at Naxos"]

THANIS: A middle-aged farmer who is also a sculptor. His beautiful daughter is named Daniella. ["Protean Challenge"]

THEBES: One of the kingdoms that King Orestes wanted to sign his League of Kingdoms peace treaty. ["Long Live the King"]

THEODORUS: One of Xena's soldiers from her early evil Xena days. He is her lieutenant, and she is romantically involved with him. Xena sends him to kill Hercules, but Theodorus fails and dies by his own sword. ["The Warrior Princess"]

THERA: Daughter of King Sidon of Syros. She is marrying Epius, prince of Delos, to bring peace between the two historically warring kingdoms. However, Thera succumbs to a spell of Aphrodite and falls in love with Iolaus. ["The Apple"]

THESEUS: A twelve-year-old boy who is sent by the dying centaur Ceridian to find Hercules. Theseus is Ceridian's youngest new protégé. ["Centaur Mentor Journey"]

THESPIUS: A prominent man of Athens whose three daughters all want Hercules to be their lover. Later, it is fifty of his daughters who chase Hercules. ["Hercules and the Circle of Fire"] ["Eye of the Beholder"]

THESSALY: A city in ancient Greece.

THOAS: On the road to Ister, he meets Hercules and reveals that Iolaus has become a victim of the she-demon. ["The Wrong Path"]

THRACE: The kingdom that the warlord Gorgus waged war on. ["What's in a Name?"] The kingdom that Maceus went to war against and defeated. ["Cast a Giant Shadow"]

TIBER: A Gargarensian man who is in love with the Amazon Ilea, but they are not allowed to be together because Amazon women live apart from the men. ["Hercules and the Amazon Women"]

TIMURON: A young, twenty-year-old man tricked to take King Sisyphus' place in Tartarus pushing the boulder up the hill unless Hercules can bring King Sisyphus back to the Underworld in three days. Timuron died on his wedding night, so he's been doubly cursed. As a spirit, he goes with Hercules and Iolaus to Corinth to confront Sisyphus. ["Highway to Hades"]

TIPHYS: A two-headed giant killed by Hercules. ["Hercules in the Underworld"]

TITANTUS: An associate of the barbarian chieftain Goth. Titantus and his band are summoned to help free Goth from Hercules at Fort Parapet. ["The Siege at Naxos"]

TITUS: A thirteen-year-old boy whose father, Gregor, has died in battle near Chaldea. Hercules is the one who must tell the boy this news. ["Ares"]

TITUS BROTHERS: Known as "big Titus" and "little Titus," they offer Salmoneus a deal to be in on their Titus family manure company. ["The Power"]

TOLAS, KING: The sickly, elderly king of the city of Alcinia. Tolas is the father of the spoiled princess Melissa and seen in "War Bride." He is killed (suffocated when a pillow is placed over his face) by his other daughter, Alexa, who has her eye on ruling the kingdom of Alcinia and starting a war with a neighboring kingdom, Lathia. ["War Bride"]

TOTH: The survivor of a village ravaged by Braxis the dragon. He's secretly selling information to Adamis. ["The Lady and the Dragon"]

TRACHIS: Hera's servant and magistrate in the small town of Pluribus. He is the one who murdered a man and woman in cold blood and then blamed the murder on Amphion. ["The Sword of Veracity"]

TRADER JOHE'S: A market stall in the village of Sarna. ["Prodigal Sister"]

TRAPPAS: A man who challenges Hercules to a discus-throwing match for charity at the Cappadocian Games. ["The Mother of All Monsters"]

TRAYUS: The second-in-command of the pirate band stalking Hercules on an island. He believes that Herc knows where the treasure is that was being transported on the prison ship. ["Mercenary"]

TREE OF LIFE CAVERN: This cavern houses the Tree of Life, the fruit of which can cure any disease with one bite. Eat the whole piece, and you become immortal. Callisto finds her way there with Hercules. During their fight, the tree burns, and Callisto is trapped there forever. ["Surprise"]

TREMULUS: He is married to Syreena, an old girlfriend of Iolaus. ["The Warrior Princess"]

TRILOS: A greedy vendor who is robbed. Thanis is accused of the crime. ["Protean Challenge"]

TRINCULOS: A thief. He shares the same dream as Iolaus and Uris to travel north, a compulsion none of them completely understands. ["A Star to Guide Them"]

TRIPTOLEMUS: A pig herder who has named two of his pigs Macaeus and Sal. He talks to them. ["The Other Side"]

TURKOS: A gladiator, one of Menas Maxius' slaves. He is defeated by Leutis but dies at the hands of the guards when Leutis refuses to finish him off. Leutis is also killed for this refusal. ["Gladiator"]

TYPHON: A sixteen-foot-tall giant held hostage by Hera. Hercules frees him and then discovers that he is the husband of Echidna, one of his greatest enemies. But Typhon is a friendly giant who is unaware of the havoc Echidna has wrecked in his absence. When he returns to her, Echidna's disposition changes for the better. ["Cast a Giant Shadow"] He and Echidna have a new baby, Obstetrius (Obie), who is kidnapped by Klepto. ["Monster-Child in the Promised Land"]

TYRON: A soldier heading home with his best friend's armor in a sleigh behind him. He tells Hercules his comrade died because he was a coward and he is returning the armor to his family. He later dies shoving Hercules and Marcus from the path of a huge boulder. ["As Darkness Falls"]

U

URIS: A farmer and the husband of Loralei. He has an infant son and older children. He shares the same dream as Iolaus and Trinculos to travel north, a compulsion none of them completely understands. He and his wife are also running from King Polonius, who is after their son because Polonius decreed all infant boys be brought to the palace. ["A Star to Guide Them"]

V

VALERUS: An archer. One of the Argonauts (of Jason fame). He is killed by one of the other Argonauts, who is a traitor. ["Once a Hero"]

VARGAS: Formerly prince of Macadamia until King Phaedron had his head cut off for speaking to him directly. ["Long Live the King"]

VEDRIS: A warrior who had fought with Hercules against Adamis. He is tricked into fighting against a dragon and is killed. ["The Lady and the Dragon"]

VEKLOS: A middle-aged miller who turns out to be Zeus in disguise. He assists Hercules' escape from an angry mob intent on revenge for Serena's murder. ["Judgment Day"]

VENALYTE: One of King Midas' partners in the Golden Touch Gambling Palace. She planned all along to cheat Midas when she had the power to dominate him by kidnapping his daughter. But Hercules intervened. ["All That Glitters"]

VERICLES: A bartender who is also a rebel in Rheanna's rebellion against King Melkos. He is killed in an ambush lead by King Melkos' captain of the army, Syrus. ["Heedless Hearts"]

VOLOS: The village near where Thanis and Daniella live. It has been plagued with many thefts and Thanis is accused of robbing Trilos. ["Protean Challenge"]

VYTOS: A villager and friend of Hercules who has lovingly tended the graves of Herc's family while Herc has been away. ["Not Fade Away"]

W

WORM MONSTER: Large creatures that live in the sand on an island and that can leap out of the sand and attack their victims. ["Mercenary"]

X

XENA: When Hercules first meets her, she is an evil warlord who is plotting his destruction. ["The Warrior Princess"] Xena shows up after Herc's wedding to Serena, only to learn that Serena is dead and that everyone, including Hercules, thinks Herc did it. She helps heal his wounds and search for the truth behind the terrible event. ["Judgment Day"]

XENAN: The young centaur son of Ephiny. ["Prodigal Sister"]

XENON: The king of Garantus, he is treacherous and plans the assassination of King Orestes. ["Long Live the King"]

XENOPHOBIUS: The father of King Oeneus, who was the father of King Orestes. ["King for a Day"]

XIMENOS: A tough street kid in Fallia who works for Atalanta, the blacksmith. He falls under the influence of Ares. ["Ares"]

XYNTHALIAN VENOM: Callisto uses this to poison the punch at Hercules' birthday party. All the guests, including Iolaus, Iphicles, Alcmene, Jason, and Falafel, suffer its effects, which include susceptibility to their wildest imaginings until they are driven mad enough to murder. The antidote is a bite of fruit from the Tree of Life. ["Surprise"]

Z

ZACHARIAH: A Macedonian who goes to kill a dragon at the behest of his lover, Cynea, but she's setting him up, and the dragon kills him. He had once fought with Hercules against Adamis, whom Cynea is secretly working for. ["The Lady and the Dragon"]

ZACHARIAS: A ten-year-old boy caught stealing apples because he's hungry. The guards, called Ironheads, plan to execute the little thief until Hercules intervenes. ["All That Glitters"]

ZANDAR: A local man in charge of the more corrupt people in Orestes. He is unearthing a treasure cave belonging to Hera, knowing full well the treasure is cursed. He is burned to death by Pyro. ["The Fire Down Below"]

ZEUS: Hercules' father and king of the gods. Zeus' favorite son, Alcmene's child, is Hercules. He risks his own life to save him in the film "Hercules and the Circle of Fire." He disguises himself as a middle-aged miller to help Hercules in "Judgment Day." In that episode, he believes Hercules is innocent of the murder of Serena.

When he learns of Strife's involvement, he gives Hercules back his powers. He appears also in "Hercules and the Amazon Women" giving Hercules bad advice about women. Zeus has trouble interfering with the gods' work, but he can change things that humans do to each other. One example is in "Outcast" when Lyla, husband of the centaur Deric, is killed in a fire set by angry bigots. Zeus brings her back to life as a gesture of good will and justice.

RESOURCES

ADDRESSES

Official Hercules: The Legendary Journeys Fan Club
411 North Central Avenue #300
Glendale, CA 91203
E-mail: outback@primenet.com

Official Kevin Sorbo International Fan Club
P.O. Box 410
Buffalo Center, IA 50424 USA
E-mail: sorbofanclub@worldnet.att.net

WEB ADDRESSES

Official Web Pages

http://www.mca.com/tv/hercules/
Universal's Official *Hercules : The Legendary Journeys* webpage

http://fastrans.net/~smiskel/KS/kevin.html
Kevin Sorbo Official Fan Club Page

http://www.usf.com/att/xena.html
Hercules & Xena: Wizards of the Screen Official Page

Fan Pages

http:msmoo.simplenet.com/guide/hug.htm
Hercules Ultimate Guide: Created by Fans for Fans

http://members.aol.com/MNicholas2/sorbo.htm
Mindy's Kevin Sorbo Page

http:www.cris.com/!msmoo/sorbo/sorbo1.htm
Sorbo Dream Page

http:universalstudios.com/tv/hercules/classicSite/vgallery/
Herc Virtual Gallery

http://vickib.simplenet.com/hercules.htm
Vicki's Tribute to Hercules/Kevin Sorbo

http://www.xenite.org/sorbo.htm
Michael's Kevin Sorbo Review

http://www.decoda.simplenet.com/HX.htm
Xenaera's Hercules and Xena Page

http://ansa.simplenet.com/cathbad/
Cathbad's Xena/Hercules Page

http://www.primenet.com/~classica/herc1.html
Democratus' Foolish Hercules Page!!!

http://www.jason.simplenet.com/actors/kevin_sorbo/index.htm
Jason's Kevin Sorbo Page

http://home.coqui.net/krystal/Kevin.htm
Krystal's Kevin Sorbo Fan Page

http://users.aol/chazthoyle/hercules.html
Hercules: The Legendary Journeys Tribute

http://members.aol.com/valsadie/page3.htm
Hercules and Xena Word Find Puzzle

Interviews

http://www.journalnow.com/living/movies/interview/sorbo.html
Interview with Kevin Sorbo

http://www.mrshowbiz.com/features/interviews/337_1.html
Interesting interview with Kevin Sorbo

http://www.pathfinder.com/people/profiles/sorbo/so
PEOPLE Online Profiles Kevin Sorbo

http://universalstudios.com/tv/hercules/classicSite/creatures/interview1.html
Interview with Creature Creator Kevin O'Neill

USENET Groups

ALT.TV.HERCULES
ALT.TV.XENA
ALT.FAN.SAM-RAIMI
ALT.FAN.BRUCE-CAMPBELL

ARTICLES

Arnold, Chuck, "Downsizing," *People Weekly,* September 1, 1997.

Baldwin, Kristen, "Hero Worship: The Record that Changed My Life," *Entertainment Weekly,* April 25, 1997.

Bufalino, Jamie, "Coming on Strong," *TV Guide,* July 15, 1995.

Gliatto, Tom, and Kirsten Warner, "Sorbo the Greek: As TV's New Hercules, Minnesota's Kevin Sorbo Gives the Mythic Muscleman a Sensitive Spin," *People Weekly,* July 3, 1995.

Jacobs, A. J., "Hercules," *Entertainment Weekly,* June 30, 1995.

Jacobs, A. J., "Kevin Sorbo & Lucy Lawless: Hercules and Xena, TV's Most Pec-tacular Duo," *Entertainment Weekly,* December 29, 1995.

Marin, Rick, "Hercules: The Legendary Journeys," *Newsweek,* June 5, 1995.

Meers, Erik, "Passages," *People Weekly,* September 29, 1997.

Rensin, David, "Lucy Lawless, " *Playboy,* May 1997.

Richmond, Peter, "Mything Links: Something Very Weird Is Going on in the Lush New Zealand World where Hercules and Xena Come to Life," *TV Guide,* November 9, 1996.

Rozen, Leah, "Kull the Conqueror," *People Weekly,* September 15, 1997.

Schwarzbaum, Lisa, "Kull the Conqueror," *Entertainment Weekly,* September 12, 1997.

Street, Rita, "Hercules Lifts Genre," *Variety,* January 15, 1996.

Tucker, Ken, "Hercules: The Legendary Journeys," *Entertainment Weekly,* June 2, 1995.

Tucker, Ken, "The Heroic Legends of Hercules and Xena," *Entertainment Weekly,* January 17, 1997.

Williams, Stephanie, and Rich Sands, "Kevin Sorbo: The Man Behind the Myth," *TV Guide,* February 1, 1997.

INDEX

I

J

K

N

O

P

Q

R

Scully X-Posed

The Unauthorized Biography of Gillian Anderson and Her On-Screen Character

Nadine Crenshaw

ISBN 0-7615-1111-3 / paperback / 272 pages
U.S. $16.00 / Can. $21.95

If you're a X-Phile, you've watched FBI Special Agent Dana Scully, M.D., advance from a supporting role to the center of the action in *The X-Files*. You stood vigil during her disappearance and apparent alien abduction—but did you know the real reason she had to "disappear"? You'll find out here, along with much, much more about both the character and Gillian Anderson, the one-time nose-ringed punk who plays the relentlessly rational Scully. Find out who Anderson really is and what she thinks of her character, costar David Duchovny and his character, the series, and other fascinating subjects in this no-holds-barred tell-all.

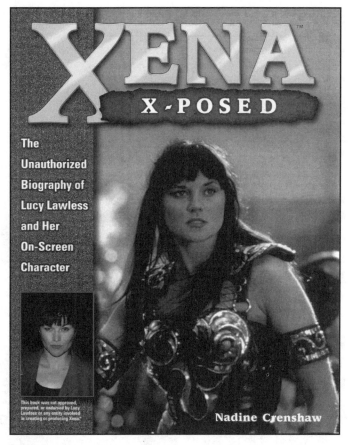

To Order Books

Please send me the following items:

Quantity	Title	Unit Price	Total
______	Scully X–Posed	$ 16.00	$ ______
______	Xena X–Posed	$ 16.00	$ ______
______	______	$ ______	$ ______
______	______	$ ______	$ ______
______	______	$ ______	$ ______

*Shipping and Handling depend on Subtotal.

Subtotal	Shipping/Handling
$0.00–$14.99	$3.00
$15.00–$29.99	$4.00
$30.00–$49.99	$6.00
$50.00–$99.99	$10.00
$100.00–$199.99	$13.50
$200.00+	Call for Quote

Foreign and all Priority Request orders:
Call Order Entry department
for price quote at 916-632-4400

This chart represents the total retail price of books only (before applicable discounts are taken).

Subtotal $ ______

Deduct 10% when ordering 3-5 books $ ______

7.25% Sales Tax (CA only) $ ______

8.25% Sales Tax (TN only) $ ______

5.0% Sales Tax (MD and IN only) $ ______

7.0% G.S.T. Tax (Canada only) $ ______

Shipping and Handling* $ ______

Total Order $ ______

By Telephone: With MC or Visa, call 800-632-8676 or 916-632-4400. Mon–Fri, 8:30–4:30.

WWW: http://www.primapublishing.com

By Internet E-mail: sales@primapub.com

By Mail: Just fill out the information below and send with your remittance to:

Prima Publishing
P.O. Box 1260BK
Rocklin, CA 95677

My name is ______

I live at ______

City ______ State ______ ZIP ______

MC/Visa# ______ Exp. ______

Check/money order enclosed for $ ______ Payable to Prima Publishing

Daytime telephone ______

Signature ______